Praise for *Humbug The Elf Who Saved*

"A perfect Christmas stocking present –
a very funny, festive page-turner"
– Jacqueline Wilson, author of
*The Story of Tracy Beaker*

"*Humbug* is that rare book: funny, original, thought-
provoking, and an instant classic" – Francesca Simon,
author of the *Horrid Henry* series

"An exquisite Christmas story, full of imagination and
heart. For the whole family to read year-after-year"
– Amy Huberman, author of
*The Day I Got Trapped In My Brain*

"You'll laugh, you'll cry, you'll need a mince pie – a new
Christmas classic" – Steven Lenton, author & illustrator
of *Genie and Teeny*

"A laugh-a-minute festive fuelled adventure full of charm
and heart. A real Christmas cracker with baubles on that

– Jam                                                            series

# STEVEN BUTLER

# HUMBUG
# THE ELF WHO
# SAVED
# CHRISTMAS

Illustrated by Kenneth Anderson

**SCHOLASTIC**

Published in the UK by Scholastic, 2022
1 London Bridge, London, SE1 9BA
Scholastic Ireland, 89E Lagan Road, Dublin Industrial Estate,
Glasnevin, Dublin, D11 HP5F

Text © Steven Butler, 2022
Illustrations © Kenneth Anderson, 2022

The right of Steven Butler and Kenneth Anderson to be identified
as the author and illustrator of this work has been asserted by them under
the Copyright, Designs and Patents Act 1988.

ISBN 978 0702 31587 9

Printed by CPI Group (UK) Ltd, Croydon, CR0 4YY
Paper made from wood grown in sustainable
forests and other controlled sources.

1 3 5 7 9 10 8 6 4 2

www.scholastic.co.uk

*For my sister, Jenny Gyertson, and all the
key-workers and valiant NHS staff.
Every last one of you is on the Good List.
Merry Christmas x*

# Chapter 1

## A Bit of a Wobbly Start

Nana Pilchard says there's a lot you can learn about a person from their name, and she's really, really, REALLY old, so I guess she must be right. Her brain is like a giant library, full of dusty information and cobwebby facts, and she's almost NEVER wrong! But, secretly ... don't tell Nana Pilchard ... if I'm being completely cross-my-heart honest, I hope she's wrong about the name thing.

I'll explain. I have the worst name in the whole world – no, scratch that – the WHOLE UNIVERSE!

You could travel from the North Pole to the South Pole and back again and not find anyone whose name is anywhere near as bad as mine. I mean it! Even if I gave you a dictionary of TERRIBLE names and loads of time to scratch your bonce and read every page, you couldn't come up with a more gunkous example.

All you Avas and Oscars and Katies and Ibrahims and Jessicas and Ravis and Rubys and Tommys and Sallys and Martins and Lunas and Archies and Fatimas out there have no idea how lucky you are. I'd give anything to be like you – all nicely-named and proud of it. It must feel wonderful.

I bet you're reading this book right now, rolling your eyes and asking yourself what on earth I'm jabbering on about, aren't you? I can picture you crinkling-up your nose, thinking, *What's this wonkling saying? No name can be that bad, can it?* and I can't say I blame you. If I was just like you, I'd probably be wondering the exact same thing, but sadly, I'm not like you. Not even close. And I know deep down in my belly there's only one way I can prove it. I'm going to have to tell you my name...

Right, are you feeling brave? Have you been to the lavy-loo and hidden yourself away someplace safe? Do you have a bucket nearby in case you get a bit blurty?

Brace yourself, my reader-friend.

My name is...

My name is...

Ugh! I can barely bring myself to say it, but I'll never be able to tell this story properly if I don't. I know – I'll whisper it.

All right, here goes... My name is Gristle.

Gristle P. Humbug to be exact (I'll tell you what the *P* stands for later).

It's ghastly, isn't it? Don't worry, you won't offend me, I already know the answer. It's the most gut-swilly, face-frowny, tongue-bleughy name this side of the Arctic Circle and it's the only one I've got.

To make matters worse, a surname like Humbug doesn't exactly make you popular with the other elves up at Santa Claus's Christmas HQ.

OH! I've just realized something... I forgot to tell you about that part, didn't I?

Ugh! Nana Pilchard always moans at me for starting stories at the wrong place, and it looks like I've done it again.

Never mind, there's no time like the present to fill you in on all the sleigh-breaking, Crimbo-cracking, lump-of-coal-licious events of my strange life recently. Are you sitting comfortably? Grab a snuggly blanket and a hot mug of cocoa, and I'll tell you everything. I promise I won't miss even the tiniest detail out.

Now, because the cogs in your human cranium might still be whirring and it hasn't quite sunk-in, I'll say it a little clearer this time. My name is Gristle P. Humbug and I am a Christmas elf. Yep, it's true! I've lived in the wilds of the frozen North for my entire frostbitten life – three hundred and seventy-six years – which means I'm still a youngster around here, but it's long enough for me to figure out how bad my first name is ... and my surname for that matter ... and my job. It's all one gigantic mess!

Don't worry, I'm not going to begin my story by

having a great big whinge-fest, but we have to start with the not-so-nice bits before we can get to the CHRISTMAS-CRACKINGLY exciting stuff.

So, here goes...

The Humbugs have slogged away at the North Pole for hundreds and hundreds of years, but we've been around for much longer, way back before Christmas even existed. We were here when the very first Santa Claus showed up ... Nikolaus, his name was ... and we've been working for the Clauses ever since.

Don't let what you've seen in books and those moving picture thingies on your human-telly-boxes fool you, though. Life isn't a wonderland of tra-la-las and tinsel for us elves at the top of the world. They don't paint the likes of the Humbug family on Christmas cards, no, sirree. We are the ones who live behind the scenes and no one wants to think about...

If you've ever spotted a picture of a Christmas elf before, it will have been a workshop elf for certain. They're the lucky ones... All cheery and giggly, practically tripping over their own round and rosy cheeks while they toil merrily. It's true! The workshoppers live up at the Big House, where Mr and Mrs Claus can keep a jolly-holly eye on the toy-making. Their days and nights are filled with nothing but happy hugs, gleeful games and mince pie parties ... but, the rest of us don't get a look-in ... not a crumb or a cuddle in sight.

I remember when I was only a lumpling of one hundred and three years, I got the cheeky chance to peek through a crack in the toy-room door when I was out on an errand for Nana Pilchard, and it's STRICTLY FORBIDDEN for non-workshop elves to show their faces around those parts of the factory.

I'd been to the store shed to fetch some dried griperoot for Nana Pilchard's pot of bedtime tea and I sneaked over to the Big House on my way back. I couldn't help risking a quick look, even though I knew I was breaking the rules.

Before my frozen feet even realized they were tippy-toeing in the wrong direction, the sound of singing and laughter practically carried me right up to that little slither of light at the edge of the enormous carved doorframe, and I peered inside.

I swear, my human reader, I'd never seen so much colour. My eyes hurt, it was so bright! Every elf was dressed in neatly-pressed spotted jerkins, poofed-out pantaloons and pointy hats with jingly bells. They were so clean and grinny, merrily beavering away, painting and hammering, chiselling and sewing the loveliest toys I'd ever seen.

It was right at that moment, as I stood shivering out in the snow, desperately wishing I could be a workshop elf, I realized that being a Humbug wasn't everything I thought it was before.

You see, the Humbugs aren't the kind of elvish family you see on wrapping paper or in storybooks or even knitted on the front of your aunty's jumpers. We don't skip around with snowmen, or twirl, or clink frosted cups of eggnog. There are NO chestnuts roasting on our open fire. We don't even have a fire to roast them on if we wanted to...

Nope! The Humbugs manage and run the R.P.D. department. Sounds fancy, doesn't it? Believe me, it's not.

"*What does R.P.D. stand for?*" I hear you ask...

Well ... brace yourself AGAIN, my human reader ... R.P.D. stands for Reindeer Poo Disposal.

Now are you starting to understand a little bit more about what I've been telling you?

While the Frosty-Frisps, and Glintles, and Patonks, and Tumfies, and McMerrypies, and Primly-Bottoms, and ALL the other workshop families dance and sing up at the big house with Mr and Mrs Claus, the Humbugs have spent the last squillion years dealing with the never-ending mountains of reindeer poo in the draughty stables on the far side of the factory.

We're not the only R.P.D. family. There are the Gardyloos and the La Trines as well, but the Humbugs have been around the longest and bear the brunt of all the hard work.

At the moment, there are six Humbugs living in our little corner of the hayloft, amongst the piles of ... umm ... you know what ... and we all get stuck in, scooping and scraping, day in, day out, as the reindeers keep eating and pooing and eating anD.. You get the picture.

Nana Pilchard and my grandpops, Old Wimbles,

tend to just sit on the hayloft steps these days, pointing and grumbling stuff like *"That needs movin'"* and *"Don't pile it downwind!"* My dad, Jiblius P. Humbug, is head shoveller, while my mum, Flotsima P. Humbug, is always armed with her buckets, ready to rush off and deposit fresh droppings into the great belching furnace that heats the mince pie ovens and the big boilers for Santa Claus's nightly bubble bath.

Then there's me and my little sister, Scratchet P. Humbug, who dash around after our parents, doing every little (and BIG) job that needs doing.

It's a poo-culiar life at the best of times, and I bet you completely agree with me about how bad my name is now, don't you?

*Gristle* is just plain dreadful. The initial *P* that's gifted to everyone in my family, whether you were born a Humbug or married into our munkled crew, stands for – you guessed it – POO! It seems my ancestors were a lot prouder of our job than we are nowadays ... and then...

And then there's my last name.

Now, I'm sure it seems that *Humbug* is by far the least terrible of the three, but it's actually the worst by far. You see, because of my family's name, I will always be stuck in the life of an R.P.D. elf, and I'll never have a chance to live in the Big House, making toys and beaming from pointy ear to pointy ear. Elves are very strict about it. You just can't do those things when you're called *Humbug*.

Ugh… What I wouldn't give to cram my gob full of mince pies and prance around, singing like a festive fool. It's a secret dream of mine, but there's no use wishing. Christmas wishes are for humans, not us elves.

I just have to face it … because of my stinky family tree, I've been doomed to an eternity of hard work and no fun.

Or so I thought … until … umm … until the day EVERYTHING changed. Yep … my life of poo, poo and more poo was turned upside down recently and nothing has ever been the same since.

I knew that last part would prick-up your non-pointy ears and make you want to hear more. Well, my human reader, let me tell you exactly what happened. It started a week before Christmas Eve…

Snuggle in and hold on tight. It's going to be a bumpy sleigh ride!

# Chapter 2

## Nights in the Stables

"Dinner's ready, my crumplets," Dad hooted. He heaved our family's dented cooking pot off the stove and plonked it down in front of us with a heavy thud. "Who's hungry?"

It was nearly midnight and all the reindeer were snoring in their stalls at last, giving us the chance to rest our aching feet and finally enjoy a spot of dinner together in the Humbug hayloft.

"I'm exhausty," my grandpops, Old Wimbles,

complained as he sat down, knees creaking like the stable doors in a blizzard. "Too much hard work. Too much blunking Christmas. Everything hurts! My joints feel like lumps of coal."

I shot a quick look at Scratchet and she smirked at me from across the table. My sister always seemed to know exactly what I was thinking, and right now it was that Old Wimbles hadn't done any work in days – he hadn't scraped or shovelled or piled-up the reindeer poo for the last twenty years to be more precise. Old Wimbles was far too ancient for any of the heavy stuff around here.

Our grizzled grump of a grandfather hadn't even clambered out of his hammock until nearly lunchtime today, and only minutes later, he'd made a huge fuss when he stepped on his own beard and quickly grumbled straight back to bed.

"Let's have a little more light," my mum, Flotsima, said with a smile, as she arranged a few candles among our empty mugs and bowls. "Make yourself useful, Scratchet, would you, dunkling?"

Scratchet nodded, then cupped her hand around

the nearest candle and gently blew on to the wick. She's always been the best at elf-magic in our family. There was an instant spark of orange and a tiny flame crackled to life, illuminating our hungry faces.

"Lovelish," Nana Pilchard said, enjoying the glow. She wrapped one of her many shawls around her, and tutted at the ice-cold draught that always seemed to whoosh around the rafters. "A few twinkly lights will really warm our clonkers, they will."

"Watch this, Nana," said Scratchet, grinning. She leaned over the table, before pursing her lips and blowing across another three candles, lighting them at the same time with a great big huff. "Ta-dah!"

"Amateurs," Old Wimbles rasped with a glint of mischief in his eye. He put down the bent fork he'd been picking his teeth with and sat up as straight as his question-mark spine would allow. "You want to see how it's really done, littlings?"

"Oh, stop your nonsense," barked Nana. "You'll hurt yourself again."

"Nonsense, you say? I used to be a champion at this in my early years. You'll see…" Old Wimbles gulped in an enormous lungful of frosty air, puffed out his cheeks, then unexpectedly spluttered in shock. "ACK-HAGH! It's freezing!"

I'm not sure what my grandpops was hoping to achieve at that moment, my human reader, but I'm pretty sure that hacking a cough and setting fire to the twisty ends of his moustache wasn't it.

"Oh, baubles!" Mum cried when she turned and spotted him. She quickly dipped her gloved fingertips into the nearest glass of water and pinched out

the two flames that flickered on either side of Old Wimbles' potato nose. "What are you doing, Pops? You'll burn the entire stable down!"

"Gerroff, Flotsima! You've soggied my jerkin."

"I mean it," Mum said sternly.

It had been a back-breakingly long day of heaving reindeer poo to the furnace and I could tell she was … well … pooped.

"Can we just have one meal without a calamity?"

But Old Wimbles had already stopped listening to his daughter.

"I'm hungerous," he groaned. "I'm so hungerous I could eat… I could eat…" My grandpops looked around for a moment, twitching his wiry whiskers, then nodded to the hundreds of reindeer snoozing in their stalls below us on the stable floor. "One of them! Horns an'all!"

"Antlers!" Nana Pilchard barked a reply as she perched on an upturned bucket.

"Yep, I'll eat the antlers too…" Old Wimbles corrected himself. "I'll gobble the lot!"

"Stop it! They'll hear you," Mum snapped at the

scraggly old elf. She was starting to lose her temper. "Honestly, we can't have you spooking the reindeer again, Pops. Blitzen is already skitterish enough as it is. You know she gets all nervous and squitsy on the run-up to the big day, and we don't want to deal with any more accidents, do we?"

"Poor Blitzen," sighed Scratchet.

"Blister?" Old Wimbles grunted. "What kind of name is Blister for a reindee—"

"Dinner is served!" Dad stopped the ancient elf mid-sentence, lifting the lid of the cooking pot with an overexcited flourish. "No one's going empty-bellied tonight."

"Oooh, that makes a nice change," Nana Pilchard cooed greedily. "What have we got? I'm ravenish!" She rubbed her grubby hands together and leaned forward, peering into the cloud of steam. "Stuffy balls with gravy, is it? Roast moose?"

"Sizzled hogglets and granberry sauce, I reckon," Old Wimbles chimed in.

Him and Nana Pilchard had spent the evening poring over a tatty human cookery book they found years ago in the bins around the back of the Big House. It was their favourite hobby. They read it so often together, ogling at and drooling over the exotic pictures, the dusty thing was practically falling apart and all its corners had gone curly. These days, most of the writing was smudged as well and they had to guess at the recipes.

"Oooh, could it be polar pig pie?" Nana asked, smacking her lips together. "I read about that just the other day, and it sounds delumptious."

"Well…" Dad pulled up another bucket and sat next to Nana. We all watched as his face drooped with disappointment. "I'm afraid… I'm afraid it's the usual."

"Not again, Jiblius!" Old Wimbles whinged. "We had *the usual* yesterday, and the day before that, and the day before—"

"That's why it's *THE USUAL*, you tinsel-brained old clodger!" Nana Pilchard bellowed, interrupting her husband and making everyone jump. "It wouldn't be called *THE USUAL* if we didn't eat it every HONKING day, would it? I'M SICK OF *THE USUAL!*"

"SHH, Mother! You'll wake the reindeer!"

Mum was the only person brave enough to tell Nana Pilchard off. She tried to look courageous as she took a seat between me and Scratchet, but we could all see the fear in her eyes.

"There'll be absolutely no more moaning tonight from any of you. Do you understand? Jiblius worked very hard rustling-up such a nice meal, didn't you, dunkling? And I think it looks … umm … I think it looks…" Mum was never very good at lying. "I think it looks really quite … usual."

"Thank you." Dad smiled at Mum, but even he didn't seem convinced by his own cooking.

Now, I know what you're wondering right now, my human reader. You're sat there imagining what kind of delightful delicacies us Christmas elves would eat every night for dinner, aren't you? I knew it! What might be our *usual*?

You're probably picturing us chomping into figgy pudding and custard, cheese and chutneys, or juicy turkey with a side of those little sausagish thingies wrapped in pig-strips – I think that's what you people call it – but you'd be wrong.

For as long as I can remember, day in, day out, us Humbugs have slurped down the same gut-grunching, throttlish slop-soup, and it looked like tonight would be no different.

"Boiled pine needles topped with hoof scrapings ... our favourite!" Dad beamed with forced enthusiasm as everyone else grimaced. "Mmmmm, smells so good." He plopped in the rusty ladle and fished out a clump of mushy twigs. "Are you hungry, Gristle?"

I didn't want to be rude, and I tried extra hard to look excited, but even one whiff of the stuff made me feel like running to the hayloft railing and puking over the side. It smelled like cabbage and nettles mixed with mud, and had the faintest sour zing of soap suds.

"Yes, Dad, I'm starvish," I replied. It wasn't a lie, my tummy was gurgling loudly after a long day of shovelling reindeer poo.

"Good boy," Dad chuckled before busying himself, filling chipped mugs with the grotsome stew and handing them out to everyone.

"I felt sure it would be some nice cheddar cheese

this time," Old Wimbles muttered wistfully. "Lovely cheddar on a crumbly biscuit. I was certain, I was."

"You don't even know what cheddar tastes like," Nana Pilchard scoffed. "Cheddar might be revoltable for all you know."

"S'not..." argued Old Wimbles. "I read about it in the book. Cheddar, I'll have you know, taste's just like ... err ... cheddar."

"You didn't read that, you great clumpus!" Nana shot back. "You're too lazish and sluggly to read."

"It doesn't matter," Mum said to her bickering parents, trying to stay calm. "I'm going to take that book away from you both if—"

Nana Pilchard clicked her fingers over the recipe book that had been sitting on the corner of the table beside her and it vanished in a crackle of light. "I don't know what you're talking about, Flotsima," she said blankly.

Mum gave up. She stared down into her mug and looked sad for a moment. "We haven't got any cheddar, Pops. I'm sorry. We've just got boiled pine needles, so let's try to enjoy it."

Everyone raised their mug of soup.

"To us," Dad said. "The Humbugs. How lucky we are."

"Close your eyes and think of mince pies," Nana declared. She said it every night.

There was a moment of quiet, until…

"I was particularly hoping for a pair of beef wellingtons myself." Nana went on, breaking the silence as she scooped steaming pine needles into her gummy gob. "They're all the rage in human parts. Hot and meaty wellingtons would be just what my sore feet need on a cold night."

"Wha's that?" asked Old Wimbles.

"Beef wellingtons?" Nana replied, tonguing bits of twig from between her last remaining teeth. "It's foodie-fashion. Those human-types love nice big beefy boots, the lucky so-and-sos." She tapped the side of her head with a stumpy finger. "Nana know these things, you see? What I wouldn't give to be one of those humans lolloping about in the warm, feasting and opening presents. That's all they do – eating and cheering and gifting each other inside their palaces. Sitting around on their big happy bottoms."

"It does sound lovelish," Dad agreed with a nod. "A life of loafing."

"Well, I think cheddar sounds better than all that..." Old Wimbles muttered to himself. "Beefy boots? What a bunch of muckbunk."

All right, let's move on, shall we, my human reader? This book isn't entirely filled with my grandparents griping over mugs of stick-filled stew, I promise.

Anyway, it was just at that moment I stopped listening to my family's squabbling and caught sight of my little sister again. She'd been unusually quiet tonight and was now wiggling her eyebrows at me from beneath her spiky fringe like she was trying to tell me something super secret.

Ignoring the rest of the chatter, I gave Scratchet one of my *Why are you wiggling your eyebrows at me?* frowns, and she winked mischievously in return. We'd become masters of silently communicating over the dinner table while our family grumbled, me and her. I tried a *Why are you winking mischievously?* frown instead and the impish rambunkler grinned back at me. I frowned one last time, as if to say *What are you grinning for?* and Scratchet finally lost her patience. She pulled a face, then banged her mug down and shrieked loudly.

Everyone stopped their jabbering and stared at her.

"What is it, dunkling?" Mum said. She placed a hand on my sister's forehead. "Are you feeling all right?"

"I'm fine, except..." Scratchet replied, suddenly looking dazed and confused. She shrugged Mum away. "It's just ... it's just..."

"What?" asked Dad. "Is the soup making you blurgy again?"

"Are you sure you're all right?" Mum repeated. She was always worrying. "You look very jitterish, my sweetling."

"GUH!" Scratchet blurted as her face creased in mock horror.

Mum and Dad always fall for Scratchet's jokes, but I could tell she was acting straightaway. What was my sneakish sister up to?

"BLOH!" she grunted. "AAAGH!"

"Something's wrong?" cried Mum.

"I... I..." Scratchet's eyes were as big as our stew mugs. She staggered up from her bucket-seat, sending it clattering across the wooden boards.

"The girl's gone clankish!" Nana Pilchard gasped, spraying pine needles in all directions. "I hope it's not catching."

"Is... Is... Is..." Scratchet looked like she might faint at any moment. She jabbed out a finger and pointed over everyone's heads to the far side of the stable. "IS THAT MRS GARDYLOO ENJOYING LOADS AND LOADS OF CHEDDAR CHEESE WITHOUT US!?!"

"Wha'?!?" Nana Pilchard and Old Wimbles were up on their doddery feet so fast they nearly flipped the table. I watched as my grandparents dashed to the railing, with Mum and Dad hurrying after them, gawping and squinting to get a good view of the

Gardyloo family's hayloft on the opposite corner of the barn.

"Gazunder Gardyloo, you greedy slobbergob!" Nana Pilchard howled over the rows and rows of snoozing reindeer, rolling up her sleeves. She'd not been a fan of the Gardyloos ever since discovering them snoozing on the job seven hundred years ago. "*Lazy-lumpers!*" she called them, and the thought of Mrs Gardyloo eating cheddar while we were gulping down pine needles clearly drove her hopscotchus with envy. "Where'd you get it, you cheddarous poopetrator? CHEDDAR-HOG!"

"Pssst!"

I turned away from all the chaos only to find Scratchet smiling at me again, looking very pleased with herself. She folded her arms triumphantly and tried not to burst into fits of laughter.

"What's going on?" I hissed as my grandparents flapped and fussed at the top of the hayloft steps. Nana Pilchard had picked up a mop and was brandishing it like a spear as she hollered across the rafters at a very startled-looking Mrs Gardyloo.

"The roof…" Scratchet replied in a whisper. "Meet me up there…"

"Huh? What's the roof got to do with anything?"

"Don't ask questions, bauble-bonce," my sister said with another smirk. "I'll see you on the roof in ten minutes…"

"Why?"

"You'll see… It's a surprise," she said. "A bungly beamish one."

# Chapter 3

## A Midnight Feast

"*B*OO!"

My little sister burst through the hole where some of the tiles had come loose, making me yelp with surprise. I'd been out in the snow for what seemed like an eternity and was feeling grouchier than Old Wimbles on laundry day about it. There was a bitter chill in the air tonight and it sliced straight through my blanket-coat, chattering my teeth and prickling my pointy ears.

"There you are, Gris!" Scratchet said as she

clambered outside. "You look half-frozen."

"I *AM* half-frozen," I humphed. My bumly-bits had gone completely numb as I sat there shivering on the icy stable roof. "You said you'd meet me in ten minutes."

"Oh, yeah, sorry," Scratchet replied with a shrug. She didn't look very sorry at all. "Nana Pilchard tried to climb over the hayloft railing for a bit of fisty-clonks with Mrs Gardyloo and we had to tempt her away with a cup of tea and a foot-rub. Bleaurgh!"

"I can't believe you did that," I said, scowling.

"Gave her a foot rub?" asked Scratchet. "I know, I'm super brave. Nana's got feet like boiled walrus blubber. I'm practically a hero. She's fast asleep now, though. They all are."

"No," I grumbled at my sister. "I mean, I can't believe you ruined our nice meal!"

"Nice?" Scratchet laughed. "Don't be bonce-boogled, Gris." She flopped into the nearest drift of snow on the slanted slates and started flapping her arms and legs to make angel shapes. "It was yuck-a-lumptious if you ask me."

"So, why'd you do it?" I was so exhaustish after a long day of work, and my little sister really knew how to be annoying when she wanted.

"I needed a cunning distraction."

"What for?" I grumbled.

"So, I could try and cheer you up," Scratchet replied. She rolled on to her side and leant her cheek against her mittened palm. "Look at you…"

"Huh?" I suddenly felt very self-conscious. "Stop it, Sis."

"You're all muttery and mopey," Scratchet chuckled. "You used to be my cheery big brother, full of jokes and jibes, but lately you could beat a gripesome old cave troll in a grump competition."

"That's not true," I said, ignoring my own thoughts as they told me she was probably right.

"Liar, liar, gifts on fire," Scratchet teased. "I spot everything, Gris. You've been a right snivelly snotling for ages, so I decided it was time to do something. That's what little sisters like me are for."

I thought about arguing back again, but I knew it was pointless. Just recently, I couldn't seem to shake this gurglish and hopeless feeling swooshing around inside me like I'd gobbled too many mugs of boiled pine needles.

"I know exactly what's wrong with you," Scratchet went on as she wriggled to her knees in the snow. "You've got the poo blues."

"Don't be stupidish."

"It's true... I've seen you, you know?" Scratchet said with a knowing smile. She had that look of mischief in her eyes again. A look she'd inherited from our nana and grandpops. "I've seen what you've been up to late at night."

My mind started to fizz as I gawped at my sister. What was she talking about?

"Sneaking out of your hammock when you think we're all snizzling away in our dreams. Tiptoeing about. I know you come up here for a right proper gruntygroan."

If my jaw hadn't been attached to my face, I think it would have fallen off and clattered down the side of the roof, my human reader. Scratchet knew my secret! HOW DID SCRATCHET KNOW MY SECRET?!?

Elves were supposed to be cheerful and bright at all times according to the strict CHRISTMAS RULES, so this was seriously embarrassing.

"Woe is me!" she gasped in mock despair, smacking the back of her hand against her forehead and pretending to swoon. "I am Gristle P. Humbug and I deserve so much more than a life of reindeer POOOOOOOOOOOOOO!!!"

Right at that moment, I wasn't sure whether to burst out laughing or melt into a blubbering puddle of tears. Possibly both?

I had been so certain that no one had ever spotted me when I ... erm... Well, you see ... I don't mind admitting, my human reader, that lately, when the rest of my family are asleep in their hammocks, I like to creep up to the stable roof to just ... I don't know ... watch the world and have a think, I guess. I'm not really a big fan of heights, but sitting up here and looking out over the Christmas Factory gave me the chance to dream and imagine my life was ... not this one. Absolutely nothing like this one...

"It's all right, Gris," Scratchet sighed. I wasn't

expecting her to do that. The mischief vanished from her face again and she placed a hand on my shoulder, giving it a squeeze. "We all want a bit more than stable life. You're not alone. Anyone would have to be tinsel-headed to wish for this."

I looked into my little sister's kind green eyes and spotted it there too … that same sadness I felt sloshing about – a sort of weary, tired, longing for something different; something a little less gloomy than year upon year of … you know what.

"I can't say I blame you for being whingerella," Scratchet said, snapping me away from my thoughts. She huffed away a loose strand of matted hair that had wriggled free from under her hat and dangled across her face, then thought for a moment. "I'd like to work in the wrapping rooms one day, I think. They always look like fun to me … all bright and colourful. I bet I'd be blunking brilliump at folding sharp corners and tying all those fancy bows as well. I'm whizzly at tying my laces after all."

We both fell silent and glanced out across the glittering rooftops of the Christmas Factory. It was a view I'd memorized for three hundred and seventy-six years and I loved it with every bit of my elvish heart.

There was something about the glow of the workshop windows, the crackle of the skating ponds, and the endless postal carts that came and went at all hours from the Great Letter Hall, that made me feel warm and cosy on even the frispiest of nights. I could stare for hours at the ghostly icicle lamps that lit the criss-cross pathways, the plumes of cinnamon-scented smoke drifting from the bake house chimneys, and the northern lights shimmering in a vast green smudge across the star-speckled sky.

Just then, a vision danced in front of my eyes. It was an elf who looked exactly like me, only he wasn't me at all; he was a different Gristle P. Humbug in a different life. My tatty clothes were gone, and in their place, the other Gristle was wearing a smart green jerkin with brass buttons and a crisply pressed collar. The holey socks that bunched around my ankles were now stripy red-and-white stockings and my hat was properly pointed without drooping to one side.

Happy tears started to collect in the corners of my

eyes. Well, if I'm being totally honest, they weren't completely happy tears, my human reader.

My dreamly vision and the view of the Christmas Factory were magnificent, but all of it seemed entirely out of reach from our freezing perch on the stable roof. I was so close it hurt. My family lived inside the walls of the most magical place on earth, but the lives of us Humbugs felt anything but magical.

"Look, Gris!" Scratchet broke the silence and pointed upwards.

I glanced in the direction she was gesturing and saw a shooting star, arching high over the nearby crooked mountains, rushing to escape the approaching dawn.

"Make a wish," Scratchet said, squeezing her eyes tightly shut. "We can share this one."

"Nah," I mumbled. "You can have it." I'd wished on enough shooting stars in the past to know they didn't listen to reindeer poo shovellers like Gristle P. Humbug.

"Stop it, stropsy!" Scratchet poked me in the arm.

"This might be the one that comes true. Make a wish, Gris."

I closed my eyes, clenched my bumly-bits, scrunched my toes and wished with every speck of magic inside me: *please, please, please make me a workshop elf. Let me make honkhumptious toys and bring a spot of joy to all the human younglings around the world. I want to be more than a stable sweeper...*

"Well, that was fun," Scratchet sighed softly when she'd finished wishing. "It's not bad up here, you know?"

"Beautiful and beamish," I agreed, trying my hardest not to let my voice tremble.

"Yep," Scratchet said. "Beautiful and beamish ... except for our squitsy corner of the factory. THE STINK BARN! This place is uglier than Old Wimbles having a nudesy soak in the tin bathtub."

Scratchet always knew how to make me chuckle.

"Anyway," she went on, "I didn't bring you up here to wail and gnash about things, Gris. I've got a present for you. Something to stop you moaning like a whoppsy worry-beast."

I sniffed away my sadness and watched as Scratchet

reached into the top pocket of her threadbare cardigan and carefully fished something out.

"What are you up to?"

"Wait for it, you impatient pook!" My little sister stuck out her mittened hand and giggled. I could see her small fist was balled around something jagged and black. "One, two, three!"

Opening her fingers, Scratchet held up...

"A lump of coal?" I groaned, feeling a pinprick of disappointment. "That's not much of a present, Sis."

Now, you should know that coal in your world, my human reader, isn't the same as here at the Christmas Factory. Not a lump of the stuff can be burned in the furnaces to heat the ovens or baths. That's what all the reindeer poo is for. Around here, coal is saved up in enormous piles and gifted to all the tantrumous human children on Santa's NAUGHTY LIST every December 25th. So, you see, it's very valuable in the North Pole, but giving an elf a lump of coal as a present is considered really quite rude around here.

"Hold your humplets," Scratchet interrupted. "I'm not finished yet. This little beautybonk took a lot of concentration to disguise, and trying to fool elvish eyes is tricksy to get right at the best of times."

Scratchet lifted her other hand to her mouth, yanked off the ragged mitten with her teeth, then wriggled her fingers over the piece of coal. "If a midnight feast doesn't cheer you up, Gris, nothing will..."

"A MIDNIGHT WHAT? We can't eat coal! YUCK!"

My eyes widened as tiny sparkles started to glimmer around the gnarled black lump. A feast? Had I heard my sister correctly?

"Almost there," Scratchet snorted like she was straining really hard.

I swear, my human reader, I wish I was able to do half the things my sister could do with her elf magic. True magic is a really rare talent at the Christmas Factory. We can all do a few charms, but elves have never been known to be terrific enchanters, not like faeries and piskies, but Scratchet was incredibump!

"You're going to love this."

*Crick, crick, crack...*

The lump of coal started to jiggle and change shape in Scratchet's palm. All of a sudden, its rough edges became neatly rounded and a crimped pattern folded itself in a loop around the top. In front of my astonished eyes, there appeared ... there appeared...

"Merry Christmas, Gris," Scratchet said with a toothsome grin on her face. She reached over and placed the most perfect mince pie I'd ever seen into my hand.

"W-where'd you get this, Scratchet?" I stammered. I was so surprised I thought my knees might buckle beneath me. In all my life, I'd never actually touched a really-real mince pie before. Such luxuries weren't for the likes of us Humbugs. We weren't important enough for pastries, even on Christmas day. I felt as though I was holding precious treasure.

"Pinched it yesterday!" Scratchet whooped, twitching her nose with glee. "The bake house was cooling a batch of fresh pies on the window-ledge and I snaffled one when no one was looking. It's been calling to me from my pocket all day."

"You pinched it?!?" I gasped. "Scratchet, you could have got yourself into trifles of trouble."

Let me make it clear, my human reader, that Christmas elves never break the factory rules. NEVER! It's our job to behave exactly as we're told and only do what's expected of us. Especially worker elves like my family.

I handed the mince pie straight back to my little sister and felt my stomach twisting itself into a knot.

"Put it back, Sis. We'll be gurniped for sure!"

"Oh, stop stressifying yourself, Gris," Scratchet laughed. She looked at me like I was the most boring elf in the world. I hate it when she does that. "No one noticed me. The bake house makes squidillions of mince pies every day for those greedy gruzzlers up at the workshop. You don't actually think they'll spot one tiny tidbit has gone missing, do you?"

"They're not greedy gruzzlers!" I barked a little too defensively. "But besides that … if you were caught, you could have been sent away into the frozen white waste like Great Aunt Abomina!"

"Well, I wasn't caught." Scratchet rolled her eyes. "I'm a really good sneaker, no one saw me, and Great Aunt Abomina actually FROWNED at Santa Claus that one time! Of course she was sent into the frozen white waste. I only squiffled a teensy snack. Just one! There's a MASSIVE difference, Gristle."

"But…"

"Enough buts, whinge-bag!" she ordered in a booming voice, doing her best Santa impression. "Ho, ho, ho! You've earned this one, Gris. Now, get it down your gobbler or you're going on the naughty list."

I didn't need to be asked twice. Before I even knew what I was doing or had time stop myself, I grabbed the perfect mince pie back from Scratchet's hand, raised it to my face and breathed in the wundumfus whiff. It smelled of nutmeg and happiness and my dream life in the Big House.

"Don't just sniff it, wonksy." Snatchet beamed. "Try a bite!"

For a second, I thought I was going to cry again. With the delunktious scent of buttery pastry filling my nostrils, I opened my mouth and took the chompiest chomp out of the pie that I could.

It was ... it was ... it was the most HUMDIFFEROUS thing I'd ever tasted, my human reader. You people-types are SOOOOOOOO lucky, lazing about all day, doing nothing but eating mince pies whenever you fancy. I can't even begin to imagine how happy you all must be.

The bite of fruity-sweety-crumbly-spicy-warmy-sticky-whoppsy tastiness jumbled my giblets and trembled my twisty-toed shoes. It was like eating happy thoughts, cosy scarves and snowball fights all in one go...

"Save some for me, greedy-grump!" Scratchet blurted when I took a second chomp. "This isn't a one-elf feast, you know?" She snatched a morsel from my tingling fingers and stuffed it greedily into her own gob, chewing slowly with a look of complete bliss on her face.

"Mmmm, it's ... it's..." Scratchet mumbled with her mouth full of pie. "It's like there's a whistling kettle in my belly."

I looked at my sister's mincemeat-smeared face and laughed, spraying her with flakes of delicate pastry crust and sugar.

"This is the best night of my life!" I jabbered through the delectable gloopy goodness sticking to my teeth and all around my gums. "THE BEST EVER! Thanks, Sis."

"Forget working in the wrapping rooms," Scratchet half-cheered, half-gulped, scooping up a handful of snow and throwing it into the air. "I want to work in the bake house from now on and grow myself a whoppsy bulging belly."

"I want to eat mince pies every day for the rest of—"

I didn't get a chance to finish my sentence, my human reader. Just as me and Scratchet were spinning around on the stable roof, mouths covered in sticky mince pie crumbs, a gruff voice from the stable-yard below cut short our fun.

"'Ere, what's all that noise?" it rasped. "Who's up there, skuttling about in the dark? We'll have no mischief tonight!"

# Chapter 4

## Misplaced Post

Frantically wiping my sugar-coated mouth on my sleeve, I peeked over the edge of the stable roof and found myself gawking at the upturned face of Swilsy Plumpaunch (Old Wimbles' best friend from elf-school hundreds and hundreds of years ago).

"I know you're up there," the jittery elf hollered as he raised a lantern above his head, squinting through thick spectacles. He was sitting on the front seat of his dented postal cart, piled high with sacks

of Christmas letters, and his face was creased with concern. "Show yourself, you rapscalliump!"

"Erm … h-hello…" I stammered, feeling my cheeks flushing red with alarm. I carefully leaned over the frozen guttering and gave Swilsy a nervous smile. "Over here, Mr Plumpaunch."

"Oh, prickle my pine cones, it's only you, Gristle," the elderly elf sighed when he spotted me. He took off his hat and wiped his brow with the back of his cuff, before fixing the rest of his ruffled blue uniform.

"You jangled my jingles, so you did."

I watched as Swilsy stooped forward and gave the enormous polar bear harnessed to the front of his cart a comforting pat on its fluffy rump.

"For a second there, me and Big White William thought we'd discovered a hoodlump causing troubles and tripe, didn't we?"

The giant animal gave a nervous growl and scuffed the snow with a spade-sized paw.

"No, no … there are no hoodlumps up here," I said, trying my hardest to look like I hadn't just been doing something I really-really-REALLY shouldn't. "It's just me—"

"And me!" Scratchet joined in. She shuffled over to the ledge and waved to Swilsy without even the slightest hint of worry on her face. "Hello, Mr Plumpaunch! Hello, William!"

"Well, I never. Gristle and Scratchet Humbug, do your nana and grandpops know you're both out in the snow at this ugly hour? Only us posties should be awake at a time like this."

"They definitely know," Scratchet lied. "In fact,

it was Nana Pilchard who sent us up here in the first place."

I glared at my sister.

"Crimbus crackers! It's been a frizzly night," Swilsy exclaimed, stroking his whiskers. "What in the snow-snaggled world did your nana send you littl'uns out on the roof for?"

"She's lost her favourite … errr … lost her favourite … umm … sock…" Scratchet went on. It was alarming how good she was at telling fibs. "A really good one without any holes or bobbly-bits. Super warm and snugglish."

"Snugglish socks on the roof?" said Swilsy, raising a snow-dusted eyebrow. "What nonkumbumps!"

"It's true!"

"Seems very oddlish to me."

"Nana thought she might have left it out here…"

"What's Nana Pilchard doing with her socks on the roof of the stable, young Scratchet?"

Christmas elves are always so nosy, my human reader, especially the ancient ones, and Mr Plumpaunch was showing no signs of giving up or moving along. Panic started pinging about inside me again and I prayed Swilsy wouldn't ask me any questions. I was SO terrible at lying. If that crinkly old fellow turned his attention back to me, I knew it would only be seconds before I was telling him everything about our stolen mince pie and we'd be banished from the Christmas Factory for ever.

"Nana likes to come up to the roof every night," Scratchet explained, giving me a jokey jab in the ribs with her elbow, "to ... umm ... to..."

"To do what?" Swilsy was looking more and more confused by the minute. "My scrumbled ears can't hear you proper from all the way down here."

"To howl at the moon!" Scratchet blurted, and I nearly fainted into the back of the postal cart below me. "She loves to just come up here in nothing but her socks and howl at the moon."

Swilsy went quiet and thought for a moment.

"Yeah," he eventually grunted with a nod. "That does sound like your nana."

My belly flipped with relief and I had to hold my breath to stop myself from whooping with joy. Scratchet truly was a master trickster EXTRAORDINAIRE!

"Oh, well then," Swilsy finally said, with a tip of his blue floppy cap. "Good luck, litt'luns. I hope you find Nana Pilchard's sock."

"I'm … I'm sure we will," I managed to mumble, feeling a jolt of excited energy at telling my first deliberate fib. It was the most un-elvish thing I'd ever done.

"Let's hope it's not been filched and sneakered away," Swilsy added as he readied himself to leave. "Strange and spine-jangling goings on around these parts lately."

My pointy ears prickled.

"Pardon?" I yelped, but the old elf had already yanked on the reins and Big White William started trudging off towards the Great Letter Hall. "Mr Plumpaunch! What did you say?"

"There's talk of a crumb-inal at large in the bake house," Swilsy shouted over his shoulder as the postal cart rumbled across the stable-yard cobbles. "Pie thief, they say! It's probably just lemmings in the larder, I reckon, but very worrying. Happy sock-hunting, Humbugs!"

I held my breath for just enough time to let the hefty polar bear pull its cargo, bumping and scraping out of the yard before turning to my sister and ... and ... I'm not proud of my language, my human reader...

"You idiumpish, pookish, bonce-boogled bungler!" I yelled right in Scratchet's face. "They know a pie was stolen! You've been rumpled! You're the most stupesy tinsel-twit in the whole factory!"

"And you're a giant wimpus," she replied with a smirk. "Stop moaning all the time."

"What if someone knows?" I started trotting on the spot in abject fear. "You heard what Swilsy said, Scratchet! There's a crumb-inal! That means they're on to you ... they're on to us ... US! I'm your crumb-inal sidekick!"

"Mr Plumpaunch said it was probably just lemmings in the larder," Scratchet muttered, shrugging. She had turned away from me and was staring at something down in the snow. "No one can catch a pie-pincher like me, Gris, I'm too sneakerly. And now we've eaten it. The evidence is squiffling around in our bellies and no one can blame us."

"But they know a pie is missing," I groaned. "What if someone in the Big House went hungry because of us? I'd never forgive myself. What if they're watching right now? We'll be pie punished!"

"Pie? What pie?" Now Scratchet was just making fun of me. "I haven't seen a pie … have you?" she trailed off mid-sentence, still staring at something a little way off in the yard.

"Maybe if we just turn ourselves in, there's a chance we might be forgiven," I said, but my little sister didn't seem to be listening. "We could insist it was a mistake, or a joke, or we didn't know... Will you look at me when I'm talking to—"

Before I could say another word, Scratchet put her hand over my mouth and pointed across the stable-yard in the direction that Swilsy and Big White William had bumped away over the cobbles only moments before.

"What's that?" she said flatly.

"Huh?" I mumbled with Scratchet's mince-pie-flavoured hand over my lips.

"That!" she said, pointing to a spot of snow in front of the tool shed. "Right there."

I narrowed my eyes and peered through the early morning gloom.

"There's nothing…"

"Follow the tracks," Scratchet ordered. "Look! It's right between them, before they pass the yard gate."

"Probably just bear prints," I grumbled angrily, but I followed the tracks with my eyes just the same. At first, all I could make out were ruts and grooves in the snow left behind by the lumbering animal, until…

"Spotted it?" Scratchet asked. There was a twinge of delight in her voice. "It must have fallen out of Swilsy's cart."

"I … umm…" My eyes fixed on something small and rectangular sticking out of the snow. It was yellow in colour and there seemed to be some writing or doodles on it.

"OUR WISH HAS BEEN GRANTED!" Scratchet whooped. "THE SHOOTING STAR LISTENED!"

In an instant I knew what I was staring at. There, right where it most definitely shouldn't be, in the middle of our stable-yard was a piece of ... of ... MISPLACED CHRISTMAS POST!

"OH, BAUBLES!!!"

# *Chapter 5*

## A Letter from Maya Pinkerton

"**Q**uick, Gris!"

I cried out in shock as Scratchet jumped straight off the roof like a cannonball in raggedy clothing and landed in a deep snowdrift that had been piled-up against the outer stable wall.

For a second, she vanished into the enormous mound with a spray of white powder, but only moments later crawled back out at the bottom, covered in snow and laughing to herself.

"Come on, wimpus!" Scratchet yelled at me as she stumbled to her feet and started patting herself down. "Hurry!"

I didn't know what to do, my human reader. I was being serious when I said I'm not great with heights. They make me feel slightly wobbly and weird. I don't even like looking over the hayloft railing if I can avoid it, but the words *LOST LETTER! LOST LETTER! LOST LETTER!* were suddenly thumping inside my head, and curiosity gripped me by the shoulders and shoved me over the edge of the gutter.

Where Scratchet had curled-up into a neat cannonball when she jumped, I plummeted towards the huge heap of snow like a flailing buzzard in a blizzard.

"WAAAOOOH!"

I hit the pile face-first and felt the sting of ice and frost on my cheeks as I sank straight into it with a sickening *CRUNCH!* The whole world turned white in an instant and it felt like someone had reached into my head and whisked my brains into eggnog. I had no idea which way was up or down until a reassuring hand reached into the snowdrift and yanked me out by the collar of my blanket-coat.

"You really are a proper clumpling, Gris." I heard Scratchet giggling. "Now, get a move on!"

Opening one eye, I found myself sprawled on the frozen cobbles, staring up at the last green shimmers of the Northern Lights before morning fully lit the sky. I was still alive... How was I still alive?

"We're going to be famous!" Scratchet blurted, before sliding her hands under my arms and hauling me to my feet.

"We ... what?" My head was still spinning and my mouth and nostrils were stuffed full of snow and ice.

"LOST LETTER, GRISTLE! LOST LETTER!"

My senses sprang straight back into focus and I spun around to face the spot where we'd seen the yellow envelope. I quickly spat out the mouthful of snow, and with it, completely forgot about our mince pie feast on the stable roof... This was FAR more important.

*

Now, in case you don't know, my human reader, there is no worse calamity, no worse DISASTER at the Christmas Factory than when a child's letter goes missing. It's the worst of the worst of the worst!

Back in 1823 a whole mail sack got lost when it fell off the back of a postal cart and slid into a cavernous crevasse. Our Santa Claus at the time, Bartholomew Claus, eleventh great-grandson of Nikolaus, was so upset, he didn't take a bubble bath for the whole month of December. Can you imagine that? Stinky Santa! Our boss – the Big Man, himself – went out on the most important night of the year, THE GREAT DELIVERY RUN, with a grubby face, smelly breath and food in his beard! It was a catastrophe of bauble-icious proportions, and to make matters worse, a whole load of human kiddlings didn't get their presents that year. It was in all the newspapers around the world. DREADFUL!

"It's coming true, Sis!" I hooted as I slipped and skidded across the cobbles, unable to actually believe a shooting star had granted a wish for someone like me. "Life at the Big House, here we come!"

I'll explain, my human reader. I don't mean I was happy that a letter had been lost, not even a little bit, but I was HONKHUMPTIOUSLY delighted that we'd found it.

You see, in a place like the Christmas Factory, throughout the centuries, letters have very occasionally been dropped, or have fallen out of mail sacks, or been plucked away on the snatcherous breeze, and it's just terrible. But the elves who recover them are celebrated like HEROES. I mean it!

Just round the corner from the stables, in the plaza between the bandstand and skating ponds, there's a golden statue of an elf named Tombulus Tibbs on a big plinth of carved ice.

*"Who's Tombulus Tibbs?"* I hear you ask... Well, I'll tell you.

Mr Tibbs worked for the S.W.D.P. department. That's the Sweeping, Washing, Dusting and Pruning department to you and me. Those unfortunate elves work and work and work just like us R.P.D.

families. They're always busily cleaning the steps and soaping the windows, snipping the bushes into fancy shapes and emptying the bins around the back of the workshops. It's bone-grunching work, but no one ever says thank you or shows any gratitude around here. No one wants to work for the S.W.D.P. department, just the same as they don't want a life in the R.P.D. stables either. So, you could say that Mr Tibbs was almost identical to me, my human reader. Exactly like me...

Anyway, one day Tombulus was sent out to shovel the paths in the middle of a terrible snowstorm that had been raging across the arctic for weeks. He was dashing back and forth like a wind-up toy, trying to keep the ways clear for the postal carts to get through, when he spotted ... you guessed it! Mr Tibbs found a misplaced letter under a frozen hedge. It had blown out of a mail sack and would have been lost for good if that valiant worker-elf hadn't been there to discover it.

The next thing Tombulus knew, Mr and Mrs Claus were holding feasts up at the Big House and he was named "ELF OF THE CENTURY!" There were parties and ballads and stories written about him, and you can bet that every baby elf born that year was named Tombulus in his honour.

Mr Tibbs lives like a king these days in his own private chalet on the crooked mountain above the Christmas Factory with a never-ending supply of cheese and chutney and he hasn't ever had to sweep or prune or scrub since.

This was our chance, my human reader! That shooting star, twinkling its way across the night, had given me and Scratchet a way out of the stables in the shape of a little yellow envelope and my feet couldn't get to it fast enough.

"They'll write carols about us, Gris!"

Scratchet reached the letter first, of course. She's always been much faster than me.

It seemed like the whole world had gone into slow motion as I watched my little sister bend down and pick the small thing off the ground.

*KA-POW!*

I knew in that instant, gawping at a yellow envelope in Scratchet's scraggly mittened hand, that our lives had changed for ever.

If there's one thing I can do better than Scratchet, it's reading words. I'm more like you humans in that respect.

There are many elves around the Christmas Factory who can't read at all, you see...

Why would they need to when they're already great at making toys or baking mince pies or folding sharp corners into wrapping paper, right?

WRONG!

Nana Pilchard insists that life is far more interesting for an elf who loves words, and I agree with her. Think how much happiness the curly-cornered recipe book has brought my grandparents over the years.

Nana's father, my great-grandpops, Crustus P. Humbug, worked in the Great Letter Hall and he taught her to read when she was barely one hundred years old, and she taught all of us in return. I've been able to read since I was only a lumpling. Nana made sure of it because she wanted me to understand all the labels on the enormous tea jars whenever she sent me to collect some from the store shed.

Scratchet, on the other hand, wasn't so great. She glared at the squiggles of writing on the little frozen envelope for a second, tried to mouth a few words, then turned it around and held it up for me to look at.

"What's it say, Gris?" she asked with wide eyes.

The writing was a bit scratchy and smudged, but I didn't have too much trouble understanding it.

"*To Father Christmas,*" I read aloud.

"Father Christmas?" Scratchet repeated, furrowing her eyebrows with thought. "It's a letter from Ingerland. That's what they call Santa there."

"Where's Ingerland?" I muttered.

"Who cares?" Scratchet was fidgeting with impatience. "Read some more!"

"*To Father Christmas, from Maya Pinkerton.*"

"Haha! Pinker-what? Humans have such gigglish names," Scratchet guffawed. "I wonder what Maya Pinkerton wants for Christmas?"

Without a scrap of hesitation, Scratchet ripped

open the envelope and plucked out the handwritten letter inside.

"Stop!" I gasped. "You can't just open Christmas post. It's for Santa to read, not us."

"Oh, clunkers!" Scratchet scoffed. "Don't tell me you're not curious, Gris. I just want to have a quick peek. I've never seen one before. We'll say the wind blew it open when we hand it over. No one will mind."

I took the letter from her with trembling fingers. This little note had the power to change our lives for ever... I just didn't know quite how much it would change things at that moment in the stable-yard.

"*Dear Father Christmas,*" I read. "*I'm very worried this year because I won't be at home in my bed on Christmas Eve. My mummy is a nurse—*"

"What's a nurse?" Scratchet interrupted me. "Sounds dangerous!"

I just shrugged a reply. I'd never heard the word before and had no idea what a nurse was.

"*My mummy is a nurse and she's got to work*

*all over the holidays without any days off. She helps*
*poorly people get better and she's a lot busier than*
*normal at the moment.*

*I'm going to be at my gran and grandad's house*
*this year instead. Can you come and find me? My*
*Gran says you will know where they live. Their*
*house is behind the big supermarket and has a green*
*front door. I hope you remember it.*

*I'm not being greedy, I promise. It's just this*
*year I'm going to give my present to Mummy, so it's*
*very important it arrives at the right place. I'd like a*
*notebook and some pens. I'm going to write a story*
*for her to cheer her up when she gets back.*

*Thank you, Father Christmas.*

*From Maya Pinkerton x*
*Flat 92*
*Greymarsh Tower*
*Trudgeworth*
*England"*

I didn't understand a lot of the words, but I

loved the way they sounded as I read them out loud. Us Christmas elves spend our whole lives working away to make the lives of you people-types jollier and jinglier, but our paths NEVER cross. I've often wondered what Christmas must actually be like. Don't get me wrong... I know elves are surrounded by Christmassy things here at the factory, but we never get to actually celebrate the really-real Christmas like you humans do. This letter was the closest I'd probably ever get to a living, breathing person ... or so I thought at the time.

"Maya Pinkerton," Scratchet said again, like she was trying out the words to see if they fit in her mouth. "Maya Pinkerton."

"We've saved Maya Pinkerton's Christmas," I laughed, feeling my skin prickle with excitement. "What are we waiting for, Sis? We have to let the Great Letter Hall know!"

"You're right!" Scratchet squealed with glee. She snatched the letter out of my hand and stuffed it back into its envelope. "That'll do... Come on! The quicker we hand it in, the quicker the feasting can start. We're HEROES!"

With that, I chased my little sister out of the yard and along the edge of the skating pond, towards the big central plaza of the factory.

"I can't wait to see our statues in the square!" Scratchet whooped over her shoulder as she hurdled a low fence. "I bet they'll be made of gold!"

She clapped and hooted, waving Maya Pinkerton's letter in the air as we rounded the ribbon dispensary and dashed through the alley between the coal shed and the bake house.

Morning was now in full swing around us and other sleepy-looking elves leaned out of doorways or stuck their heads through windows to see what all the fuss was about.

"Wha's all this?" A grease-smeared elf asked us as we clattered past the open door to the sleighworks. He was sitting on the front step, cleaning a rusted wrench on the sleeve of his tatty overalls before a hefty day of repairing and polishing. "You squiblings are racketous this morning. What's occurrin'?"

"We found a letter!" Scratchet guffawed back at him, waving it proudly. "WE FOUND A LETTER!"

The elf looked like he'd just been slapped around the face by an entire sack of Christmas post, and before long he and many others had taken chase behind us.

"Look, over here!"

"Quick! There's going to be a party, I bet!"

"Come and see!"

"Well, I never!"

"WOO-HOO!!!" It was all so exciting, my human reader. Happy thoughts were cascading through my head at such a rate, I barely noticed the large posters that had been nailed to the side of the wrapping room and hung on the stripy wooden posts of the bandstand as we passed them: brightly-coloured signs declaring, *PASTRY PINCHER AT LARGE!* and *HAVE YOU SEEN THIS PIE?* and *WHO'S BEHIND THIS CRUMBLY CRIME?*

Nope, with so many elves cheering us on as we passed, I hardly even realized that Scratchet hadn't turned towards the Great Letter Hall as we crossed the plaza, but was running straight for the Big House instead.

"Sis!" I blurted as we rounded the bandstand and I finally noticed she was straying off course. "Where are you going, Scratchet? Stop!"

"We'll get you that dream job in the workshop, Gris," Scratchet hollered without slowing down. "You'll be head toymaker by lunchtime!"

"What do you mean?" I huffed, trying to keep up. "You're going the wrong way!"

"Oh no I'm not," Scratchet replied, jumping and skipping as she went. "We're taking this letter right to the top!"

We couldn't disturb the Big House, could we? I had no chance of reaching her. Scratchet was way too fast for that, and even if I could catch up with the mischievous imp, she'd wriggle free and do it anyway, I just knew it.

With Maya Pinkerton's letter still held above her

head, I watched my little sister bound up the steps to the Big House, three at a time, and make a dash for the giant bell that hung on a huge brass hook near the top.

Normally, the bell was only used for proper emergencies, like when one of the workshop elves was hungry or they'd run out of buttons or beads, but that didn't matter to Scratchet.

She jumped into the air, grabbed hold of the bell-rope with her free hand and swung back and forth like an overexcited orangutan.

*CLANG! CLANG! CLANG!*

# Chapter 6

## CRUMB-INALS!

*I*n no time at all, a crowd of curious and gossiping elves gathered around us on the steps in front of the Big House. Below us, more and more factory workers were wandering over from the ribbon dispensary, coal sheds and sleighworks; familiar nosy faces, all gawping and jostling about, trying to get a better view.

What was even more gut-gurglingly exciting, my human reader, was the commotion happening above us on the veranda at the top of the steps.

No sooner had Scratchet swung on the emergency bell, the huge carved doors at the base of the Big House started to creak open and I could see right into the heart of the toy workshops. Machines clanked, spinning wheels whirred, and clockwork conveyor belts carried rows of dolls and teddy bears through the centre of the vast room, thronging with clean and happy elves.

I had to squint my eyes as colourful lights spilled out on to the snow-covered cobbles, and even though it was already morning and the sun was up, they tinted everything with jewel-like sparkles.

"WAIT!" a shrill voice cried out from somewhere inside the doors, and I spotted an elf – dressed neatly in a yellow-and-pink spotted jerkin and poofed out pantaloons – sprinting out towards us. "What in a thousand frozen Fridays is going on? Who has DONGED the emergency dinger? This is an outrage! Only I am allowed to do that!"

I had rarely seen this squirrelly little elf in all three hundred and seventy-six years of my life, but I knew who he was almost immediately, with his extra-coiffed eyebrows and a clipboard clutched tightly under one arm. Unless I was very much mistaken, I was looking at the factory foreman – Bungustus McMerrypie.

My stomach did a cartwheel beneath my blanket-coat. I was about to meet the manager of the whole workshop. This was it! He would be my new boss in the not too distant future, so I needed to make a good first impression.

"Well?" the elf whined as he skittered out on to the veranda, before seeing the crowds of workers looking up at him from the plaza and flinching with surprise. "What is the meaning of this gathering?" His startled eyes darted about as he tried to understand this unexpected interruption to his day. "Why aren't you all working? We don't have time for practical jokes and lollygoggling around here! There's only a week until the big da—"

It was at that moment that the foreman spotted me standing on the top step. He flinched again and gave me a look as if to say *"DON'T COME ANY CLOSER!"*

"You! Stable elf!" he snapped at me with a hint of

a sneer at the corner of his mouth. "Are you the cause of all this chaos? Why is no one working?"

"Excuse me … erm … hello…" I stammered. The McMerrypies were an extremely old elf family and I couldn't believe I was standing before the most important of them all. I took off my hat and felt my face turning as pink as Bungustus's polkadots. I couldn't wait to see the delight on his face when he learned about the missing letter. "It's a real pleasure … umm … that is … I'm very glad…"

"Who are you?" a voice asked from somewhere above us, interrupting my stammering.

Bungustus McMerrypie glanced upwards and let rip with a theatrical scream when he saw Scratchet dangling from the emergency bell, flapping her patchwork coat about her like the sail of a tatty ship.

"IT'S A PLAGUE OF STABLE WORKERS! This is most irregular," the foreman shrieked as he staggered backwards, dropping his clipboard into the snow with a look of horror on his face. "You shouldn't be here. Shoo! Shoo! Go back to where you came from!"

"Sorry," Scratchet giggled, before letting go of the

bell and dropping to the ground. "I didn't mean to judder you, Mr?" She waited for him to say his name.

"How rude!" Foreman McMerrypie looked incredibly insulted when he realized that Scratchet wasn't joking – she really didn't know who he was.

"I said," Scratchet went on, "I didn't mean to judder you, Mr?"

"I'll have you know that you are addressing

Bungustus Plugbert Aubrush Plonkulus McMerrypie! Two hundred and thirty-fifth generation of Christmas Factory foremen, and you should know exactly who I am, young man!"

"I'm a girl," Scratchet said, looking puzzled.

"You are?" McMerrypie backed another step away. "It's hard to tell anything about you under all that grime. Why are you dressed like a boy?"

"I'm dressed like a Scratchet, actually," my little sister humphed.

"Bleugh…" Bungustus looked as though he might be sick.

"We need to talk to the boss," Scratchet went on, completely ignoring the jittery elf's less than kind comment. "It's super important."

"I *am* the boss," the foreman said coldly.

"No, you're not." Scratchet laughed. "Haha! You don't look anything like the boss. Your beard's not big enough and he definitely doesn't wear spotty—"

"Yes, I am THE BOSS," Bungustus shot back again. "I manage the factory floor like a well-oiled cuckoo clock. There's not a toy in the whole place that doesn't end up in Santa's sleigh without my say-so."

"Ooooh!" Scratchet laughed again. She extended a hand for Bungustus to shake, but he refused the offer and took another step backwards. "We may have some crossed ribbons."

"What do you mean, stable … thing?"

"When I said we need to talk to the boss, I meant *HIM UPSTAIRS* … you know?" Scratchet pointed to Mr and Mrs Claus's private apartments that sat on top of the workshops above us. "We need to speak with Santa right away."

Bungustus gawped at my little sister like she was dressed up as a giant turkey and pecking seeds out of the snow.

"Just a moment." His face twisted into a mocking smile. "You are telling me that you broke the rules and dinged the emergency donger…"

"Last time, you said 'donged the emergency dinger'," Scratchet cut in.

"Quiet!" Bungustus's curly eyebrows started to twitch with frustration. "As I was saying, you are telling me that you ... ahem ... rang the bell because you want to chat with ... with Santa Claus himself?!"

"Yes, Mr McMerrypie." I stepped forwards, mustering any courage I could from deep inside me. "It's hugely important that we speak to Santa. You see, we've found something."

By this point, lots of other workshop elves had shuffled over to the great carved doorway and were huddled together, each a perfect family portrait in their colour-coordinated uniforms. They all stared at me and Scratchet like we ... it was hard to read their expressions ... like we didn't belong.

"These workers," Bungustus had turned to face the workshop families and I could hear in his voice that he was about to make fun of us. "They want to talk to Santa Claus! They just popped over from the stables, covered in muck and mottlies, for a quick natter and a cup of tea, it seems."

My heart sank like a stone through a fishing hole as the workshoppers all started to laugh. No, not just laugh ... they were pointing and laughing, and everyone knows that's the absolute worst kind. This wasn't how it was supposed to happen. This was the moment my dreams were going to come true and they'd all welcome me into their wonderful world of lights and toys and mince pie parties.

"Santa doesn't have time to stop for the likes of a pair of stable stubs!" Bungustus jeered at me and Scratchet. "Now go back to where you came from and don't bother us again. Next time, it'll be the frozen white waste for you both."

I wanted to curl up like a dead leaf and blow away on the spiteful wind, my human reader. Bungustus McMerrypie was completely right. How on earth could I have been so stupid to think that Santa Claus or any of the other HONKHUMPTIOUS workshop families would ever see me as anything but...

"Laugh all you want, you grinning pack of gruzzlers!" Scratchet hollered, causing a hubbub to ripple about the busy plaza below us. "You won't be laughing for long."

Bungustus, who had swished around and was striding back towards the Big House, froze in his tracks.

"What did you say?" he turned so slowly it would have made icebergs look speedy. "I didn't quite hear that, young man."

"I told you, I'm a girl!" Scratchet humphed.

"You're a *THING!*" Bungustus roared dramatically. "A rude, grimy little thing who clearly has no idea that an elf like you should never be in the company of elves like us. As I said before, go back to your stables and stay away."

My heart sank even further when I saw nods of agreement from the workshoppers still huddled in the doorway.

"But…" I muttered. It was all I could manage. Why was I such a wimpus?

"What was that?" Bungustus snapped.

"But we found … we found a…"

"Speak up or is your gobblet too full of reindeer poo?" This was followed by more chuckling and whispering from the workshop elves.

"We…" I could hardly say a word. "We…"

"WE FOUND A LOST LETTER!" Scratchet shouted. She struck an impressive pose and thrust

Maya Pinkerton's yellow envelope into the air. "NOW BRING US SNACKS AND CARVE OUR STATUES!"

To say that Bungustus McMerrypie looked a bit shocked would be like saying the North Pole was only a bit chilly.

"Oh, my blessed baubles!" he croaked and practically bowed as all the other workshop families rushed out into the snow and gathered around us, trying to get a better view, just like all the worker elves in the plaza below. "Forgive me, valiant young workers, I had no idea!"

"That's more like it," Scratchet said over the group as they pushed and heaved behind their foreman to get as close to us as possible. "What was that you were saying about stable stubs?"

"A mere slip of the tongue." Bungustus laughed nervously. "Just a Christmas joke!"

All around me were faces I'd memorized since I was a kidling. Toymaker heroes of mine, and I couldn't believe they were now struggling and shoving to come and meet me and my little sister.

"Where'd you find it?" Scurrily Pudgenut from

the woodcarving division asked, and I nearly fell over with elation. Her wooden alphabet blocks were world-renowned. "You must be proud as puddings."

"Well done! Well done!" Ariazmus Bunt, bookbinder extraordinaire, clapped and hooted. "You've saved the day."

"I'm going to make a duo of dolls in your likeness," Crotchety Humpkins beamed at us both. The very fact that she was looking at me made me feel somewhere between fainting and vomiting. Miss Humpkins was SO famous. No one could make a doll that wet its frilly pants better than she could.

"I think this calls for a celebration," Bungustus announced, quietening down the busily chattering elves around us. He waved his arm and they all stepped aside, then he ushered me and Scratchet over to the edge of the veranda.

My heart was pounding so loudly it filled my ears and I struggled to hear what the factory foreman was saying as he turned to address the crowds below us.

"Ladies and jubblyjims!" he declared as the whole factory compound fell silent. "After a teensy-weensy misunderstanding, it has come to my attention that this pair of … erm … elves from a lovely corner of our home … umm … that is, the stables, have found a lost letter!"

A roar of approval went up over the mass gathering. Every elf in the factory must have been down there looking up at us. I scanned the faces for my family, but I couldn't see them anywhere. I hoped they were watching. Mum and Dad would be so happy.

"As you all know," Bungustus went on. "We elves always follow the rules, and our CHRISTMAS RULES state that a feast must be held for any elf who finds a misplaced letter, even when we are dangerously close to the big day and the elves in question are … umm … a bit … not like us."

I glanced over at Scratchet and saw her grinning from ear to ear as she waved at people. Why wasn't I feeling the same? Something about Bungustus McMerrypie made me feel nervous.

"So, without further ado, I declare…" The foreman turned to Scratchet and raised his curly eyebrows.

"SCRATCHET P. HUMBUG!" Scratchet yelled with pride.

"Yes … umm … I declare that Scratchet P. Humbug and…" He turned to me and I told him my name. "And Gristle P. Humbug will be known henceforth as ELVES OF THE YEA—"

Bungustus gasped so loudly I thought he was going to inhale his moustache. He reached up and seized the lapel of my hole-ridden coat, and I looked down in time to see his finger jabbing at a constellation of mince pie crumbs that were stuck in the rough threads and snags of fluff.

"You!" he hissed in my face. "You're the…"

# Chapter 7

## Crime and Punishment

"CRUMB-INALS!" Bungustus McMerrypie's cheeks turned the colour of holly berries as he yanked me towards him and bellowed across our captivated audience in the plaza. I swear to you, my human reader, I've never had much to lose in my life as a Humbug, but seeing my hopes and dreams of being a celebrated workshop elf crumbling before my eyes felt like I'd been kicked in the guts by a rampaging reindeer.

"You!" Bungustus said again, only this time it

was a roar. "You thieving RUMPSCALLIONS! You stealsome little snatchlings! You tweaking, sneaking, pilfer-pooks!"

By now the cheers of happiness from the crowd had diminished to a low and very confused burble. I looked out over the factory compound and felt panic and shame swooshing through me. This was a NIGHTMARE!

"Christmas elves, one and all!" Bungustus shouted to the throng of faces. "There has been a twist in the tinsel!"

"Oooooh!" the crowd oohed in unison.

"These stable stubs of the family Humbug have deceived us all!"

"No, we haven't!" Scratchet protested. She held up Maya Pinkerton's envelope again and waved it. "Look! We really did find a letter in the snow. It fell off the back of Swilsy Plumpaunch's postal cart. WE SAW IT!"

"Silence!" Bungustus snapped. "Seize them!"

Two burley workshop guards lumbered forward and grabbed me and my little sister by the shoulders.

They were HUGE by elf standards: employed heavies to keep the toy rooms safe from snitcherty fingers and snoopsy eyes. I tried to wriggle free, but it was no use. You see, I may be lots of things, my human reader but strong is not one of them. I was stuck there, forced to stare out over my gathered community, feeling worse than I've ever felt in my life, and that's including the time I fell off the hayloft steps into a freshly shovelled mound of *you know what...*

"Yesterday, a terrible crime was committed. Dreadful wickedness, the likes of which I thought no elf could ever perform," Bungustus went on. I could tell he was really enjoying himself and being extra dramatic. "A poor defenceless mince pie was pinched from the bake house by a mysterious villain. One unfortunate workshopper had to go without their nap-time snack!"

"It's too rotsome to think about!" an elf from the ribbon dispensary screamed as she practically crumpled on to her friend's shoulder.

"Who could do such a thing?" shouted a stout

elf from the wrapping department. "It's got me all a'tremble."

"Elves don't pinch things! There are rules," wailed another. "This can't be right?"

Bungustus puffed out his chest and drew himself up as tall as he could (which wasn't very tall at all).

"Ah, but it *is* right," he announced gravely, before jabbing a stubby finger in my face. "With these sharp factory foreman eyes, I spotted crumbs on this pilfering pest's clothing."

The crowd gasped and I found myself desperately hoping that Mum and Dad were not watching. What would they think of me? They'd never speak to me again, and I'd deserve it too.

Bungustus raised the collar of my coat to his nose and sniffed.

"Butter … cinnamon … a hint of clementine… IT'S UNMISTAKEABLE! WE HAVE FOUND THE CRUMB-INAL!"

"Leave Gristle alone," Scratchet yelled, kicking and struggling in the workshop guard's arms. "He didn't do anything. I stole the pie. It was me!"

"You're all as guilty as one another," Bungustus sneered. He looked at us like we were utterly pukeable. "Do you know the trouble you Humbugs have caused?"

He turned and pointed to a very angry-looking Crotchety Humpkins. Her kind smile seemed to have dropped off into the snow and something told me she wasn't planning on making a set of dolls in our likeness any more.

"Poor Miss Humpkins missed out on her fourth mince pie at last night's party! There just weren't enough to go around."

"I only took one!" Scratchet exclaimed. "It's not like you greedy gruzzlers are going to starve, is it?"

Everybody looked horrified, and Crotchety Humpkins sauntered towards us with an air of disgust about her.

"Look at 'em," she hissed, eyeing me and Scratchet the same way I look at a mug of boiled pine needles with hoof scrapings. "Coming over here ... stealing our mince pies."

Two other elves from Crotchety's famous doll-making team ran to support their friend. Primpy Patonk and Jinkly Rolly-Poll. I'd idolized them for years and years, and couldn't believe quite how badly our first meeting was going. I always imagined we'd be friends...

"Stable stubs are different to us workshoppers," Jinkly Rolly-Poll said, grimacing. "I don't think they're even real elves at all."

"Send them away, Bungustus," whinged Primpy Patonk. "Anywhere but here. They're not the same as us and I don't like it!"

More shouting erupted from the gaggle of workshop elves in the doorway. Names were called and heads were shaken.

I was just contemplating curling up into a ball with embarrassment, when...

"What the blunking bungersnipes is going on 'ere?!" A voice blurted from somewhere in the crowd below. "Move your bumly-bits. Let me through or I'll fisty-clonk every last one of yer!"

I watched as the overexcited throng parted and Nana Pilchard marched towards us with Mum, Dad and Old Wimbles hurrying along behind her.

"Bungustus McMerrypie, you moansome mountain goat! What are you doing with my grandkiddlings?"

Hearing my gnarled old nana speak to the factory foreman like that filled me with a mixture of complete shock and … well … I suddenly found myself having to stifle a nervous giggle. If anyone could sort this mess out it would be Nana Pilchard. I'd prayed my family weren't watching this whole ordeal unfold, but now they were here, I couldn't help but feel relieved. Maybe things wouldn't turn out quite so badly after all.

"Oh, look," Bungustus groaned. "More Humbugs. That's just what we need."

"Don't you be givin' me cheek, young man," Nana warned, wedging her fists against her hips. "You tell your brutes to let go of Gristle and Scratchet or I'll come up there and give you a smacked rumpus, I will."

"These elves have committed a whoppsy crime, Miss Humbug!"

"Oh, hogswash! And it's MRS HUMBUG to you! My grandkidlies have done nothin' but scrape and clean and work so that you and your pampered pals don't have to." Nana scoffed. "Have your eyebrows been curled too tight, you great wonkling?"

Bungustus flinched and raised a finger to one eyebrow to check everything was perfectly in place.

"Stop this muddling, right now," Nana went on. "Look!" She pointed to her tapping foot to show the factory foreman exactly how impatient she was. "I won't be tellin' you again. I knew your mother, young man. You're not too old to be sent to your bed without a single blunking snack, make no mistake."

"Don't talk to me like I'm a lumpling," Bungustus cried.

If I'm not mistaken, my human reader, I think I saw his bottom lip trembling.

"Right, that does it," Nana Pilchard said flatly. "Now you're in for it, you sassified stropling."

With an enormous grunt, Nana Pilchard hoicked up her skirts and aprons and started trudging up the stone stairs towards the Big House.

"I'm not havin' you bully my littl'uns," she wheezed as she climbed. "I'll make sure … ugh … won't be a moment…" She hauled herself up a few steps, paused for breath, then hauled herself up a few more. "You'll regret this, you… Phew … it's hot … just a minute… I'm going to tell Santa what you … ugh… Just wait there … I won't be a jiffy … huh … whuh… You'll regret this when I … ugh…"

By the time Nana reached the top of the steps, every elf in the factory was staring in silence. I could see Mum and Dad whispering to each other at the foot of the staircase and I knew exactly what they were saying. Dad would be wanting to go and help Nana before she exploded, and Mum would be warning him that he'd get a bonk on the head if he dared to offer her the slightest assistance. Old Wimbles on the other hand was fussing with a hole in his cardigan and I don't think he'd even noticed anything out of the ordinary was happening.

"Now you're in fer it," Nana panted as she finally stepped on to the veranda.

"I'm sorry," Bungustus said, trying to hide the fear on his face. "There is nothing you can do, Mrs Humbug. We have caught these hooligans hot-fingered, I'm afraid. They are pie thieves and therefore must be punished."

"Stop talking such grot and gripe," Nana replied. "My kiddlings are good'uns. They ain't got time to be snitching pies. The stables keep us all far too busy to be fussing about with your pastries."

"The youngest … erm … thing has already admitted it." Bungustus nodded towards Scratchet.

"Your hat's on too squeezy." Nana smirked. "My Scratchet wouldn't—"

"It's true, Nana," Scratchet interrupted. "I took the mince pie and ate it. I must have dropped crumbs on Gristle's coat. It's my fault, not his."

Nana's mouth fell open in a shocked gape.

"Please, Mr McMerrypie, you have to let Gristle go," Scratchet pleaded. "He's a good elf, and he really did find a letter, and he wants to work for you, and he'd be great at making toys, I just know it!"

"Pah!" Bungustus laughed at my little sister, and it made me feel crosser than I'd ever felt in my life. "You think we'd allow a stable stub into our lovelish workshops?"

"Send her to the frozen white waste!" Jinkly Rolly-Poll squealed.

"Send all the stable stubs away!" Primpy Patonk agreed.

"Who are you calling STABLE STUBS?" Nana growled. "Even if … even if…"

"Reindeer got your tongue, Mrs Humbug?" mocked Bungustus.

"Even if my Scratchet did steal a pie from the bake house … who could blame the poor little grubling? We're starvatious down there in that blusterous barn, we are. You lot clink your mugs and nibble your nibblies up here, while we're scrapin' and carrying poo to the furnaces, day in, day out. The ovens wouldn't even work if it weren't for the likes of us."

"That's not the point!" Bungustus stuck his fingers in his ears. "La! La! La!"

"Why can't you workshoppers share?" Nana barked at the gaggle of elves crowding behind their foreman.

"It's not our fault you're hungry," Crotchety Humpkins shot back. "You should work harder and maybe you could move up in the factory."

"WORK HARDER!?" Nana gawped. "We couldn't work harder if we tried. You lot should share the pies!"

"You shouldn't even be on our nice clean and tidy side of the plaza," said Primpy Patonk. Had she not listened to a word my grandmother had said? "Stick to your side of the bandstand!"

"It's only clean and tidy around here because of them," Nana pointed to a team of S.W.D.P. elves who were busily sweeping a little way off. They all looked up from their work, startled. "I bet you don't share any mince pies with those elves either!"

There was a moment of stunned silence from the workshop elves.

"We ... well, we..." Bungustus muttered, clearly searching for something to say. "We don't need to share our mince pies with the S.W.D.P. department, because ... well ... because we occasionally give them a round of applause and they much prefer that to ... umm ... food..."

I watched as Nana fumed like a stubby volcano. Mum, Dad and Old Wimbles had made it to the top of the steps by now and they shuffled in around her like people sidling up to an unexploded bomb.

"Just breathe, Mother," Mum whimpered at Nana. "Why don't we all just take a second to—"

What can I say, my human reader? Nana didn't

take a second to do anything. Just when I thought things couldn't get any worse, I watched in slow motion as she rolled up her sleeves and...

*WALLOP!*

# Chapter 8

## A Plan

"I just can't believe it," Mum blubbed. We were back at the Humbug hayloft and everyone was standing around in a state of shock, shuffling our feet and mumbling to ourselves. "The frozen white waste! The frozen white waste, Jiblius!"

"I know, dunkling," Dad soothed Mum with wide eyes. "I know…"

"What are we going to do?" Mum started flapping about, hurrying from one side of the loft to the other and back again.

Now, I know you'll be wanting all the gory details of what happened, won't you, my human reader? It's quite simple really. Nana did the best and most sensible thing that she could think of to do in that moment of stress and surprise. Yep! She biffed Bungustus McMerrypie right on the end of his squirrelly nose, sending him flailing backwards and knocking over the entire workshop team in one go. They all went down like skittles in pointy hats and a decision was made very quickly indeed after that.

The family Humbug was banished! Kapow! So long! Ta-ta for now! Wish you weren't here! Remember not to write!

A whole battalion of workshop guards dragged us all back here and told us to be out of the factory by midnight tonight.

I clambered into my hammock and lay there facing the stable wall, feeling… I don't even have the words to describe how I was feeling. In one giant splat, I'd lost my dream of making toys in Santa's workshop,

I'd been branded a crumb-inal, and I'd been ordered out of my home to go and wander in the frozen white waste for the rest of my life.

"Maybe we could find Great-Aunt Abomina?" Dad said, hopefully. "We could build a shelter, or we could become fishermen of the polar deep? You always wanted to try mackintoshes didn't you, Nana?"

"Mackerel!" Nana huffed back.

"We haven't got a boat, Jiblius." Old Wimbles croaked. "And I don't like the sea ... it's too wet if you ask me. If water was dry ... lovely ... but it's not for me and my clunkerous knees."

"I should've whumped McMerrypie harder," Nana Pilchard grumbled to herself from her seat on an upturned bucket. "Teach that squeary scoffler a proper lesson."

"That's quite enough from you, Mother!" Mum snapped. "Look what you've done!"

"He was being rudesy about our family," Nana replied. "I won't have him calling Scratchet a sneaker and a filcher."

"But it seems HE'S RIGHT!" I'd never seen Mum so angry. She turned her pale and tear-streaked face towards Scratchet. "Why did you do it, dunkling? You know not to steal. YOU'RE AN ELF! How could you put your whole family in danger for a pointless mince pie?"

"Mince pies aren't pointless, Flotsima!" gasped Old Wimbles. "They're not!"

"That doesn't matter now, Pops," Mum sighed. "I just don't understand, Scratchet. What in the worlds did you do it for?"

Scratchet looked around the hayloft at us all and shrugged.

"I just wanted to cheer Gristle up," she said. "It was only meant to be a bit of fun. I didn't think it could hurt to surprise him."

"That's right," Nana agreed, defending her granddaughter. "Scratchet was just bein' kind, weren't you? Besides, I used to pinch pies all the blunkin' time when I was a nipster. The trick is not to get caught…" She gave a rattly laugh and looked very proud of herself. "Scratchet deserves a pie every now and again, and so does Gristle."

"Well, things certainly feel a bit hopeless, don't they? I hope it was a delicious treat," said Dad. "Let me think... We'll have to pack up the essentials, and bring the cooking pot, and—"

"I wish we were humans..." The words just came out of my mouth, quite unexpectedly. All my life, I'd loved being an elf at Santa's Christmas Factory, but that was only when I thought I could one day become a workshopper and spend my days making dazzling and brightly coloured toys for you humans.

In that moment, I was feeling extremely rattled at how mean the workshop elves had been. I always thought they would welcome me with big smiles and armfuls of hugs, but now that dream had been well and truly grunched, I suddenly thought about how brilliant the life of a regular person would be ... far away from the North Pole and all these reindeer.

"Me too, m'boy!" Old Wimbles chuckled. "Me too."

"And me," Nana Pilchard cooed. "Nothin' but food and gifties and sitting about on your bot-bot in a cosy palace. It's much better than being an elf, I've heard."

"Not now, Mother," Mum said as she started folding up blankets and shoving them into a cloth bag.

"I mean it, Flotsima," Nana went on. "Think about it … us elves spend the whole year preparing and toiling and making and scraping Christmas together, but we never actually have Christmas, do we? That's only for humans. They're dunking their heads in chunkolate fountains and snacking on cheesy cracklers while we're working our tootsies into nubs and bumples."

"Those lucky so-and-sos," Old Whimbles wheezed.

"Well, we don't have time for wishing right now," Mum said. She was clearly still furious. "Everyone, start gathering your belongings and—"

"HANG ON A MINUTE!" This time it was Scratchet's turn to interrupt.

We all turned to stare as my little sister started digging around in the pockets of her jerkin.

"I nearly forgot in all the whoppsy drama," she mumbled, tapping and exploring each pocket, until…

"A-ha!" Scratchet held up the yellow envelope from Maya Pinkerton like it was the answer to all our problems. "Why don't we go and be humans for a change?"

"Don't be tinsel-brained, Sis!" I said. "Elves can't just go and be humans."

"Why not?" Scratchet replied. She turned to the rest of our family and held the letter out for everyone to see. "We weren't lying."

"Oh, baubles," Mum groaned. "You mean if you hadn't stolen a pie, you really would be Christmas heroes by now? This is worse than I thought."

"Yes ... but ... erm ... no ... that's not what I'm saying," Scratchet said, scrunching her face as she thought up a plan in her head. "This letter is from Maya Pinkerton."

"Ha! What a daftus name," Old Wimbles snorted. "Why can't humans have normsy names, like Bogruss or Raffelty?"

"I know," Scratchet continued. "But that's also not what I'm trying to say ... even though you're right... People-types have seriously laughabus names. Anyway, Maya Pinkerton wrote to Santa because her nurse-mumsy has to work in a hop-spital over Christmas and she's not going to be at home..."

"What's a hop-spital?" asked Old Wimbles.

"I know this," Nana Pilchard cut in. "It's where very sleepy people go to lie in bed for a long snoozy time, and those nurseys bring 'em treats and wash 'em and tuck 'em in at night. Ooh, those humans are lucky."

"Sounds lovelish!" Old Wimbles said with a wink.

"Shhhh, you two!" Mum was clearly losing her patience again. "Can you please get to the point, Scratchet."

"So," Scratchet whooped. "As I was saying, there's a house in Ingerland that's going to be empty for the big day."

It took me a little while to catch up to my HONKHUMPTIOUSLY-minded sister, but as the cogs in my cranium started to whir, I began to understand what she was saying.

"And?" Dad said as he wrapped the family

cooking pot in old rags to keep it safe. "What does that have to do with us?"

"We know that all humans live in palaces filled with food and fun, right?" Scratchet explained. "And we know from Maya Pinkerton's letter that hers is going to be completely empty. It's called Greymarsh Tower, and it's waiting just for us."

"I love towers!" Nana Pilchard hooted.

"I'm thinking we go for a holly-day," Scratchet said. The mischief had returned to her eyes. "We can pretend to be humans and people will bring us gifts and nibblies and mountains of mince pies—"

"AND CHEDDAR CHEESE!" Old Wimbles nearly fell over with the gusto of his cheer.

"I've heard the buildings are made of cheddar cheese, Pops!" Scratchet beamed. "And there are rivers of chutney, and everyone sleeps on pillows made from puffed marshmallow."

"Gosh! That would be wonderly," Dad sighed. He glanced at Mum and I could see they were both giving Scratchet's idea some serious thought. "We've never had a holly-day before."

"A new life as a human..." Mum thought out loud. "No more shovelling and carrying buckets to the furnace."

"Nothing but putting your feet up and snacking," said Scratchet. "We've all earned it."

"Blunker's to this place," Nana Pilchard blurted. "You can count me in, young Scratchet. What do you say, Flotsima? Jiblius?"

Mum and Dad gave each other one last look before they both slowly nodded. Then all eyes turned to me.

"How about it, Gris?" asked Scratchet, and for the first time in days and weeks and months, a big, bungly and bright feeling of happiness went pop in my belly and I found myself grinning a really-real teeth-and-all grin.

# Chapter 9

## The Getaway

"Which one do you reckon?" Dad asked as everyone gathered on the hayloft steps and puzzled over the rows and rows of reindeer, snizzling away in their straw-filled stalls. We'd waited nervously all day, fussing and chattering, but finally night had crept back around and it was time to put our plan into action.

"We need a nice old one," Nana Pilchard mused, scratching her bumpy chin. "One who's been out on the Great Delivery Run lots of times. I can't be doing with no jumpsy beginner. Geoffrey maybe? He's a big old bungler. Dasher is a good runner too."

"I'm not sure about this," said Mum, having second thoughts. "We've already been banished to the frozen white waste and branded pie thieves today."

"Exactly!" Nana replied with a nod. "While we're already in trifles of trouble, now is the perfect time to borrow a reindeer as well."

"That's not what I meant, and you know it, Mother," Mum muttered. "Isn't there another way we can get out of here?"

"Not unless you want to walk to Ingerland," said Scratchet, shutting Mum up in an instant.

"This is going to be tricksy," Dad said. He tapped a finger thoughtfully on his lower lip and hummed to himself for a moment. "I was thinking Snuffler myself ... or Betsy-Lou. No?"

"Snuffler's too ... snuffly," Old Wimbles complained. "And Betsy-Lou dribbles..."

I bet I know what you're wondering right at this moment, my human reader. You've heard the famous poem about Santa and his reindeer and you're thinking something isn't sounding quite right, aren't you?

Well, I can tell you here and now, the poem only named a handful of the delivery run reindeer, and those ancient fellows from the first team retired yonks and yonkers ago.

We still have some of the great-great-great-great-great-great-great-great-great-great-great-great-great-great-great-great-great-great-great-great-great-great-great-great-great-great-great-great (I think that's nearly correct) grandkids of Nikolaus's original flying squad, but there are hundreds of others in the stables as well. The last time I counted there were over eight hundred reindeer in our care. Now can you understand why there's SO MUCH POO?

Each and every one of the reindeer is pampered and preened in its own warm stall with more delicious food than us Humbugs could ever wish for ... and they only work one day of the year. Come to think of it ... maybe I'd like to be a reindeer from now on...

*

"I'll know the perfect beast when I see it," Nana Pilchard announced. "Follow me, my dunklings." And with that, she led us into the aisles of reindeer stalls, stopping at each nameplate like someone perusing items to buy in a shop. "Nana knows best."

"Just keep your noise down," Mum demanded in a hushed voice. She pointed up to the Gardyloo's hayloft on the other side of the stables and we could clearly see them all sitting down to a dinner of boiled pine needles with hoof scrapings, just like we would have been if ... you know... "We mustn't draw attention to ourselves."

"Oh, blunkles to the Gardyloos," Nana Pilchard grumbled, waving her hand about like she was swatting flies. "Let's find the right reindeer and get our *derrières* in the airy-airs."

"Grotsy?" whispered Dad as we passed his stall. "He's energetic."

"Too stubborn," Nana replied. "And he smells."

"How about Comet?" said Mum. "That would be nice and traditional."

"I don't like the way she looks at me, that one,"

Nana grumbled. "And I'm sure I heard her mooing the other day. It ain't right!"

"Reindeer don't moo, Nana," I said, trying not to laugh.

"Comet does. Mark my words, Gristle. She's a right moo-er."

We wandered up and down the rows of sleeping animals for what felt like ages and ages, keeping to the shadows and out of sight from the Gardyloos and the LaTrines.

"Mother, this is taking too long," Mum snapped at Nana, but the hobbling elf was showing no signs of being satisfied.

"Stomper's a good flyer," Dad said, over-enthusiastically.

"His fur's scruffy."

"I like Blizzard Bolt," Scratchet added.

"Nah, that one's got devious nostrils."

"Dancer?"

"Too fancy..."

"Sky Skipper?"

"She's knock-kneed! Look!"

"Wind Skimmer?" I read aloud from another nameplate.

"Windy-pops Puffer, more like."

"Cupid?"

"He's a bit bitey…"

"Jupiter?"

"Too runty…"

"Prancer?"

"I don't like her attitude…"

"Star Shooter?"

"Bleugh!"

"Vixen?"

"How dare you? I hate that one… I feel like she's judging me…"

"Snorter?"

"Nah!"

"Beverly?"

"Have you seen the size of her head?"

"Storm Sailor?"

"Too greedy…"

"Tripper?"

"I've never trusted that one…"

Back and forth we went with Nana rejecting every reindeer we came to, until we reached the end of the last row and the very final stall. Peering inside, everyone stared at the wonky-antlered reindeer who had fallen asleep with her head stuck inside her feeding bucket. Her snoring echoed out of it and made her sound like she was half reindeer and half battered-old-gramophone, just like the one Mrs Claus listens to.

"Blister!" Old Wimbles declared. "There's only Blister left."

"It's Blitzen, Pops." Scratchet smirked. "Remember? We talked about her last night at dinner."

"That's what I said," Old Wimbles grumbled. "Blister! It was a stupid name last night and it's a stupid name now. Does no one listen to me?"

"Well, we can't possibly take Blitzen," Mum said with a shake of her head. "She's skittish and squitsy at the best of times. She's totally wrong for the job."

"She's my kind of reindeer," Nana Pilchard hooted. "And a family name that goes right back to the original eight."

"But we can't take *THIS* Blitzen!" Dad yelped. "Last time she led the Great Delivery Run, Santa ended up in Australia!"

"What's wrong with that?" Nana Pilchard huffed. "Humans have Christmas down there too."

"They were aiming for France!" Dad replied.

"I like her," Nana said, ignoring Mum and Dad completely. "She's a reindeer who knows where she wants to go. She's like me in a lot of ways."

"S'right," Old Wimbles agreed, putting a loving arm around his wife's shoulder. "We'll get to this Greymarsh Tower of yours with a courser like good old Blister leading the way."

"But she gets lost, Pops!" Mum tried to reason with her parents. "She never listens to what she's told."

"So, we'll tell her we're not going to Greymarsh Tower, and then we'll head straight there. I trust her!"

Blitzen jolted awake at the sound of all our chitter-chatter, then lifted her head with the metal food bucket still stuck over her nose and half a hay bale caught in her antlers. She yawned loudly then flopped on to the floor and rolled over with her hooves in the air.

"All those in favour of Blister?" Old Wimbles asked, raising his hand over his head, along with Nana.

No one else put their hands up...

"That's unanimous then," said Nana Pilchard with a contented nod. "Blister, my old chum. You're coming with us..."

One hour and quite a few bumps and scrapes later, we had managed to wriggle Blitzen into her harness and lead her out into the night without being seen by the other R.P.D. families or demolishing half the stable, although there were times when it seemed like we might do both.

"We mustn't be spotted!" Mum kept whimpering every time the clumsy reindeer knocked over a barrel or scraped her wonky antlers along a wall, which only made everyone feel all the more nervous. There were, after all, still a few worker elves hurrying about at this late hour and the postal carts wouldn't stop coming and going all night.

I swear to you, my human reader, at the risk of sounding … well … a little bit boring, I suppose, I really hadn't ever had an adventure before that trembulus day. It all felt terrifically nau … naug … ugh! It's hard for me to even say it. "Elves are not supposed to be NAUGHTY (there, I said it), and it was thrilling to see how rebellious Nana Pilchard was. She was like some kind of elvish superhero.

"I wish I could see their faces when I send Bungustus McMerrypie and that ratsy little Crotchety Humpkins a postcard from our new life at … what was it again?"

"Greymarsh Tower, Nana," I said.

"At Greymarsh Tower," Nana Pilchard cheered.

"Shhhhh!" Mum looked like flames might shoot out of her ears at any moment. She clearly didn't have the same rebellious streak as her parents.

"All right, dearie." Nana Pilchard soothed Mum with a gap-toothed smile, before whispering, "Don't get your panty-bloomers in a twist."

We slipped as quietly as we could from shadow to shadow around the ribbon dispensary, with Blitzen clattering and clomping behind us, then headed between the bake house and coal shed.

"It's not far now," Scratchet encouraged us in a hushed voice. She pointed to the hulking shape of the sleighworks looming ahead of us. "We'll be out of here in no time." And she wasn't wrong, my human reader...

It took an enormous amount of heaving and huffing to get the massive rusted door to the sleighworks open. By the time everyone was safely inside and me, Mum and Dad had managed to shut it again, Nana Pilchard had already clambered into ... I couldn't believe my elf-eyes... There I was, pushing and tugging to close the mighty door, when I turned and saw Nana sitting in the driver's seat of ... of ... THE SLEIGH!

SANTA CLAUS'S ACTUAL SLEIGH!

It was a beautiful thing to behold, and so much bigger than I had expected.

Don't get me wrong... I'd watched Santa take-off on the Great Delivery Run lots of times from my perch on the stable roof, but I had never seen it this close before. The elf craftsmanship was exquisite. Red-painted cedarwood, delicate carvings of Alpine forests

on both sides, polished brass runners along the bottom, a padded seat of woven bear wool, and a handy cup holder for Santa's magical never-ending mug of eggnog. I thought I might burst out crying at the sight of it.

"Oh, yes! I could get used to this," Nana Pilchard beamed as she waggled her stumpy feet back and forth against the driver's seat. She'd already grabbed Santa's flying goggles from the shelf at the front and had yanked them down over her eyes, making her look like a squat, round insect. "Let's go, Humbugs!"

"Mother!" Mum shrieked as quietly as she could. "What are you doing? We can't take the ACTUAL Christmas sleigh!"

"Why not?" Old Wimbles grumbled. He was halfway up into the seat next to his wife, but had got stuck, and now dangled over the edge of the huge red vehicle like a bony-legged rag doll.

"Don't be such a party-poopcicle, Flotsima," Nana said, yanking the reindeer-less reins and pretending to steer. "I think red suits me."

"Flotsima's right, Nana," Dad joined in nervously. "If we take THE sleigh, the whole of Christmas will be ruined. No child on earth will get their present and all the children will stop believing in Santa, and it will be … it will be our fault."

"Good!" Nana barked. "That'll teach that bearded bozo for putting someone like Bungustus McMerrypie in charge, won't it?"

"Enough!" Mum suddenly erupted with her THERE'LL-BE-NO-MORE-BACKCHAT-FROM-ANY-OF-YOU voice. She was the only person brave enough to use it on Nana. "Get down here this instant, Mother, and we can look at some of these other sleighs. There are lots, see?"

Nana Pilchard didn't move…

"NOW!" Mum demanded.

"Oh, all right," Nana finally groaned. "But I'm keeping the goggles!" She dropped the reins and started clambering awkwardly from the high seat, a mass of crumpled skirts and waggling feet. "Don't look at my bumly-bits!"

# Chapter 10

## Into the Bright Beyond

"It's perfect!" Nana clapped her hands together and jumped up and down with glee. "This is the one!"

Just like choosing a reindeer, we'd spent far too long wandering up and down the rows of sleighs and everyone was getting twitchy.

"We need to hurry up," fretted Dad.

"These things take time, Jiblius!" Nana scolded him. "Besides, I've found it now, haven't I?"

The sleighworks was enormous and filled with

half-built or broken vehicles. They ranged from huge postal carts and toy transport trolleys, right down to the super speedy messenger sledges used by flight-controller elves on the night of the Great Delivery Run. Nana, of course, had said "No" to each and every one of them – *It's too wide... We can't be seen in something THAT piddly... I don't like the colour, it clashes with my shawl!"* – until we'd all but given up. Maybe we just weren't supposed to ever escape our fate in the frozen white waste?

I was busy scuffing my feet and wondering if there was any way I could apologize to Bungustus McMerrypie – an *I'M SORRY* letter, maybe? A bouquet of polar pansies? – when Nana squealed happily.

There she was, looking more like a pile of discarded laundry rags in her extra winter layers, standing in front of ... of...

"Mother, that's a dumpster!" groaned Mum.

"Lovelish!" Nana beamed. "That's the one. I knew it was as soon as I laid my peepers on it, I did."

"But it's horrible, and rusty, and ... not a sleigh

at all! We can't fly out of here in that. It's a deathly clap-trap!"

"It's just what we need," Nana said with a grin as she gestured at the large wheelie bin like a magician's assistant. "It's not too poshly, just like us Humbugs … and I can't be doing with any of that fancifuss, *tra-la-la* honkswallop. This one is sturdish, and it's got all four wheels, look. Those little trundlers will make light work for dear ole Blister. What do you think, my wonksy four-legged chum?"

Nana Pilchard turned to where Blitzen was nosing at a pile of lumber in the corner and the skittish creature grunted back at us.

"What did I tell you? Blister loves it!"

"That was just a grunt," Mum protested. "You don't speak reindeer, Mother!"

"Ah, but it sounded like a very positive grunt," Nana replied. "Very yessy, if you ask me."

"How in the worlds can you tell that?"

"I just know these things," Nana tapped the side of her head with a stubby finger. "I've told you a zillion times."

"She has!" Old Wimbles piped up in defence of his wife. "It's true, Flotsima!"

"That's settled then," Nana said with a contented nod. "Gristle! Jiblius! Give it a push, will you, dunklings? Get a move on!"

I looked at Dad and he pulled a face as if to say *"We'd better do what she says"*. If there's one thing we've all learned when it comes to Nana Pilchard, it's that arguing rarely gets you anywhere. Dropping the strange doohickey I'd been examining back into a nearby toolbox, I rolled up my blanket-coat sleeves and readied myself to push Nana's wheelie bin out into the icy darkness.

It's hard for me to remember exactly what happened next, my human reader. The closer we got to actually leaving the factory, the more I started to panic. I hadn't even been outside the walls before! I'd never seen the big wide world, or flown with a reindeer, or had a single night away from the stable in all my three hundred and seventy-six years. What if we were just heading to our certain doom in a deer-powered wheelie bin?! My head was swimming with all kinds of fears and hopes and doubts and worries, and it combined to make one gurglish cocktail of confusion inside my bubbly brain.

I know me and Dad must have pushed the bin out of the sleighworks and over to the factory airstrip that ran alongside the skating ponds, but I can't recall even a moment. It was like my memories had turned to smoke and blown away on the frosty wind like Maya Pinkerton's lost letter. I was in a total daze, and the next thing I remember, was glancing upwards and seeing that my family were now huddled together inside the dumpster with Nana at the front, clutching on to Blitzen's reins, and squabbling with my grandpops.

"You can't have second thoughts now, you dodderous whump-wit!"

"It's just..." Old Wimbles griped. "It's just..."

"JUST WHAT!?"

"Well..."

"Spit it out or we'll have to leave you here to scrape piles of poo all on your lonesome."

"I DON'T TRUST SOUTHERNERS," Old Wimbles blurted. "Never have … never will!"

"WHAT?" Nana was clearly furious with the disruption to her impressive dumpster take-off, but the big goggles she'd pinched from Santa's sleigh made her look wild-eyed and completely peculious, and I caught Scratchet trying not to laugh.

"We live in the North Pole, Grandpops," my sister said, smirking at the pair of cantunkerous elves. "Everyone in the world is a southerner to us."

"Exactly!" said Old Wimbles. "I don't trust their funny ways down there in warmer parts. I heard everyone walks on the ceiling and they sleep with their feet in the air, the weirdy-woos! My Great-Uncle Grumple told me."

"That's just factory gossip," Scratchet said. "Nothing but wafflings and whispers. You sound like one of the snobsy workshop elves."

"They're not snobsy!" I gasped. I wasn't quite ready to admit I may have been a bit wrong about the elves in the Big House. I still wanted to believe that the workshops were a wonderful place. "They're the best!"

"You could have fooled me." Scratchet rolled her eyes. "The workshoppers are a bunch of snob-a-licious bullies! And all this talk of not trusting people because they're different or they're workers is just a load of garbish!"

"I agree, Scratchet, my lump," Nana Pilchard said, as she fussed with the strap of her goggles. "Now, that's enough of this carbunk."

"S'not carbunk!" Old Wimbles grumbled at us. "Southerners *are* weirdy-woos! My Great-Uncle Grumple heard it from an elf in the wrapping department, who'd heard it from her mumsy in the bake house, who heard it from her friend in the Great Letter Hall, who overheard it in the queue for the store shed. How can that be gossip, I ask you?"

"Nonkumbumps, Pops!" Nana Pilchard snapped at her husband. "Stop your gripin', you whiny old wobbler and shut your whiny old gobbler!"

My grandpops closed his mouth at once and frowned.

"That's better," Nana said, trying to hold her temper. "Are we all in and comfy-like?"

"Yes," my dad answered, his voice betraying a hint of fear. "We're all in … and … sort of comfy. Is this thing safe, do you think?"

"It couldn't be safer, Jiblius, but in the event of an emergency," Nana continued with confidence, "exits are … umm … anywhere…"

"But how do we know it's even going to fly?" Mum asked. She grabbed my hand, then Scratchet's, and squeezed us both tightly. "You've never steered a flying sleigh … er … bin before, Mother."

"Oh, stop your worry-warting, Flotsima," Nana said. She didn't seem to be concerned at all. "How difficult can it be? If Santa can do it, I definitely can. I've watched that bearded berkle do it loads of times."

"But it might be dangerous!"

"Dangerous?" Nana scoffed. "We're big and brave Humbugs! We don't worry about danger, daughter. Besides, what could be dangerous about flying through the air in a dumpy-bin thingy with

Blister at the helm? She's a professional! We're all safe as snug-bug-rugs, I'd say."

With that, Nana took a deep breath and lifted the reins in front of her. "Are you ready, Blister?"

Blitzen was busily chewing on stray bits of pond grass poking up through the snow. It didn't seem like she'd even heard the be-goggled driver behind her.

"She's ever so ready," Nana informed us all. "I can tell." We all held our breath and watched with wide eyes as my grandmother gave the reins an almighty snap. "GIDDILY UP, BLISTER, MY LOVE! DASH AWAY! DASH AWAY! DASH AWA— OI! I SAID DASH, YOU GREAT BUNGLER!"

Nothing happened...

Nana shook the reins again.

"GO!"

Blitzen ignored her, munching on arctic weeds instead.

"Move your rump-lumps, you lazy horse with horns!"

Still Blitzen did nothing. She looked up at Nana

and seemed extremely confused – if reindeers could be extremely confused.

"Get ... A ... Move ... On!" With each word, Nana yanked and flicked the reins, jerking and twisting this way and that like a demented spinning top. "Why ... Won't ... You ... Fly?"

It was just at that moment, we suddenly heard—

"'Ere! Wha's going on over there?"

Everyone turned to see a workshop guard emerging from the darkness of the plaza with a lantern held over his ham-sized head. It was one of the big burly captains who'd helped to drag us all back to the stable after our embarrassing showdown with Foreman McMerrypie earlier that day.

"Who's out causing a ruckus at this late hour?"

"Oh, blunkers!" Nana yelped. She turned back to Blitzen and started shaking the reins even harder. "Come on, Blister, my beauty-toot!"

"Mrs Humbug? Is that you?" the workshop guard was making his way around the edge of the ribbon dispensary. "And is that ... IS THAT A REINDEER!?"

It wouldn't take him long to run around the skating pond and wrestle Blitzen's reins from Nana's squidgy grip.

"Blister! If you don't get us out of here now, there'll be no lovely life in the nice warm human world to look forward to. Just the frozen white waste! You'll have icicles for antlers if you don't hurry!"

I'd never heard Nana sound frightened or panicked before and it shook me to my bones, my human reader. I was used to the cold, but my teeth started to chatter, nonetheless.

"Go, Blister! PLEASE!"

Everyone gawped as the guard drew closer.

"Don't mind us, good sir!" Nana called over her shoulder to the thuggish brute in a strange poshified accent. "We're just taking Blister out for her evening exercise. She loves a good trot, you know?"

"It's over," Dad whimpered under his breath. "We're done for."

"I told you we should have brought more blankets," blubbed Mum. "We're going to need them out there in the frozen white waste. We'll be snow elves by morning!"

"I'll never get to try cheddar now!" Old Wimbles wailed.

"STOP WHAT YOU'RE DOING!" the guard commanded behind us. He'd reached the skating pond and, instead of running around it, was attempting to wobble his way straight across it, slipping and sliding as he went. "RELEASE THE REINDEER! SOUND THE ALARM!"

Somewhere across the plaza, we heard the emergency bell being *donged*.

"STAY RIGHT WHERE YOU ARE!"

It was terrible, my human reader. All in one day, I'd lost my dream of becoming a workshop elf and now the promise of a new life in the human world was also crumbling by the second. I glanced at Mum and Dad as they flapped about, then turned to Scratchet who ... who didn't look worried at all. Not even a bit!

"Nana," my little sister said in a voice that was startlingly calm. "Don't forget Blitzen is a bit like you!"

"Eh?" Nana snorted as she thrashed about with the reins. "Beautifulsy? Intelliump?"

"No! Bad at following orders," Scratchet corrected her. "She doesn't listen, remember?"

"Scratchet P. Humbug, you little brainy-bonker," Nana cheered, before turning back to Blitzen. "DON'T GO, BLISTER!" she barked. "DON'T YOU DARE TAKE OFF WHEN I'VE TOLD YOU NOT TO GO ANYWHERE."

Blitzen lifted her wonky-antlered head again and stared at us with wide blank eyes.

"YOU STAY RIGHT WHERE YOU ARE, BLISTER!" Nana barked, making the reindeer flinch. I could almost hear the cogs whirring in Blitzen's furry bonce. "NO RUNNING! NO NOTHING, DO YOU HEAR? DON'T MOVE A MUSCLE, BLISTER! THERE'LL BE NO FLYING TONIGH—"

*WHOOSH!*

Blitzen was off in such a hurry I nearly toppled out of the dumpster on to the snow below. If it hadn't been for Scratchet grabbing me by the scruff of my blanket-coat and heaving me back, I'd have been left behind on the side of the skating pond for certain.

"Haha!" Nana whooped, coughing and spluttering

as the wind started to whip our faces. "DON'T GO, BLISTER! STOP! STOP! STOOOOOOP!"

Twisting her head this way and that, our bewildered steed went clattering across the frosty ground in a one-deer stampede.

"WOO-HOO!" Nana howled in delight. She snapped the reins, encouraging Blitzen to sprint as fast as she could. "NAUGHTY, BLISTER! DON'T TAKE OFF!"

In seconds Blitzen's legs were a blur. Hooves thundering, nostrils snorting clouds of warm air as she tore along the airstrip, dragging the Humbug-stuffed wheelie bin behind her like it weighed absolutely nothing.

"DON'T DO IT, BLISTER!" Nana cackled as our reindeer ran faster and faster. "SLOW DOWN, GIRL!"

The bin bumped and skidded. Sparks exploded out from the rusted wheels below us and there was an ear-jangling squeal of metal, until...

Silence...

Well, not quite silence, but almost. Suddenly

the banging and grinding of the bin stopped, the drumming of Blitzen's hooves on the hard earth faded and we were left listening to the whistling of rushing air as we ... as we...

Squished between Mum and Scratchet, I wriggled around to face the back of the dumpster and watched with tear-streaming eyes as we FLEW!

"Oh, chunksome chimneypots!" Mum yelped. She gripped my hand so tightly I could see her knuckles turning white. "I'M NOT SO SURE ABOUT THIIIIIIIIIIIIIIIIIIIIIIIIIIIIIIIIIIIIIIIIIIIIIIIIIIIIIIIIIIIIIIIIIIIIIII..."

The airstrip sped away beneath us at a ferocious speed and the entire factory emerged into view as we climbed higher and higher into the snow-filled air. There was the angry guard shaking his fists at us from the middle of the skating pond, there were the shimmering rooftops of the ribbon dispensary, the bake house and the coal sheds.

"TA-TA FOR EVER!" Nana Pilchard guffawed as she jerked on Blitzen's reins and guided us in a wide curve over the factory compound. "BYE, BAUBLE-BRAINS!"

Below, as the emergency bell still tolled, I could see the speckled lights of lanterns appearing as elves from all departments rushed out into the night to see what new commotion was occurring.

"Look, Gris!" Scratchet pointed as we raced high above the wonky roof of our old home. I saw the Gardyloo family running into the yard, dressed in their stripy nightgowns, agog at the airborne bin scudding over their heads.

"See you, stink stables!" Scratchet laughed, waving and cheering. "We'll miss you!"

"NO, WE WON'T!" Nana cackled when she spotted the Gardyloos as well. "Gazunder Gardy-poo won't be able to laze about while we do all the work any more!"

Guided by Nana Pilchard's swervy steering, Blitzen swooped over the wrapping department, narrowly missing the sleigh-shaped weathervane, before rocketing around the bandstand and across the plaza towards the Big House.

"WHOPPSY WIDE WORLD, HERE WE COME!" hooted Nana. "NO MORE HARD WORK! NO MORE BOILED PINE NEEDLES!"

She steered the speeding dumpster straight towards the glowing shape of the workshops and the Claus's private apartments.

"AND NO MORE NORTH POLE!"

We all watched as startled faces appeared at all the Big House windows and Bungustus McMerrypie ran out through the slowly opening doors to the toy rooms. He was followed on to the veranda by Crotchety Humpkins and her gaggle of mean elves, and they all screamed and scattered in different directions when the sight of Nana Pilchard in a fast-moving bin hurtled towards them.

"COWARDLY CONKS!" Old Wimbles blustered as we careered overhead. "FRAIDY-FRUMPS!"

I'd be lying if I said it wasn't completely thrilling, my human reader. These elves had been incredibly unkind earlier in the day and the look of shock and surprise on their faces as we WHOOSHED upwards, clearing the corner of the building was deliciously funny to see.

But that wasn't even the best bit!

Just as we zoomed higher, hurdling the last of the

Big House's turrets, I took one last glance backwards and saw... Were my eyes playing tricks on me? NO! There on the top balcony of the Claus's private apartment, was ... was ... Santa himself. The Boss! THE BIG MAN had come outside and was watching us make our escape with his mouth hanging open like a stupefied codfish.

The rest of my family were all looking to the front of the bin to watch the approaching skyline, nattering and jostling about, but not me... I stared at the glowing sprawl of the Christmas Factory until it diminished behind us into nothing but a pinprick of light in the wilderness. My home. The only place I'd known for three hundred and seventy-six years was gone in a flash.

"It's beautiful," I heard Scratchet sigh, and I looked in the direction we were soaring. There was another dawn amassing in the distance beneath the green smudge of the Northern Lights, and as we all stared in nervous, excited silence, the horizon yawned and we flew straight into it.

# Chapter 11

## "Southward! I Think…"

"We're going the wrong way." Scratchet finally plucked up the courage to say it. "We should have turned right at Bulgium."

"How do you know what Bulgium looks like, you young backy-chattling?" Nana Pilchard scoffed as she heaved Blitzen's reins this way and that. "I just saw Old Zealand back there."

"Don't you mean New Zealand?" Mum asked. She'd been growing increasingly green-looking the more we swooped and dived and zigzagged through the clouds.

"No, I don't!" Nana barked, blinking at us through her human-sized goggles. "Old Zealand is nothing like New Zealand! It's dustier, with a hole in it and a few more cracks around the top bit."

Scratchet caught my eye at that moment, then shrugged and pulled a face.

"I think you might be confusing countries with something else, Nana."

"Ugh! It's hot," Old Wimbles groaned, joining in with all the complaining and fanning himself with a gnarled hand. "Are you sure this is right, my dunkling? I didn't expect Ingerland to be so ovenly."

"Leave me to my steering, the lot of you." Nana said through gritted teeth. "I know exactly where I'm going. We've just passed Old Zealand, and Ingerland is over the next hill, right next to Eeegypt where the pointy houses are."

"We're in India, Mother!" Mum snapped.

"India ... Outdia ... I don't CAREDIA! I know

exactly where we are," my grandmother said, absent-mindedly adjusting her goggles again as they steamed up. "We are not in India!"

"But that's the Taj Mahal!" blurted Mum, pointing to a vast marble palace-like building as it sped away beneath us. "We're in India. I did a project all about it at elf school when I was a nipster."

"Cor!" Dad cooed, looking instantly happier as he sweated in the heat. "Is that what all human homes look like?"

"Yep!" Nana replied over her shoulder. "When we get to Greymarsh Tower, we'll be spoiled rotten with luxurly luxuries."

"I can't wait," Dad beamed. "Our first ever family holly-day. I love you all, you know? We're so lucky."

"We won't be very lucky if we don't turn Blitzen around and head in the right direction."

"I won't tell you again, Flotsima," Nana humphed. "Look! There's Ingerland!"

Below, the arid land had swiftly given way to green and lush hills as we raced through the morning air like a wonky comet that had drunk a little too much

Christmas punch. I looked ahead to see Ingerland, but saw Nana Pilchard was pointing towards a gigantic and impenetrable mountain range that was tearing towards us.

"Those are the Himalayas!" Mum practically screamed. "Blitzen can't cross those!"

"Don't be dafticles." Nana laughed. "There's no such place as the Him-a-wotzits—"

"Will this help?" Old Wimbles interrupted as he took off his tatty cardigan and a large scroll clattered out of it, landing on the floor of the dumpster with a loud metallic *CLONK!*

"What's that?" asked Mum. She carefully bent down in the tight space and fetched the cylindrical object from between Old Wimbles' slippered feet.

"I found it," my grandpops muttered, instantly looking a bit sheepish.

"You found it where?" Mum narrowed her eyes suspiciously and unrolled the scroll a little.

I peeked over her shoulder to get a better look at the fancy thing. Each of the ornately carved ends were topped with golden baubles, frosted with sparkling snowflake patterns, and as Mum unravelled it, I could see the parchment was covered in squiggly lines and words with lots of arrows coming from them.

"OH, CRUMBLES!" Mum yapped with alarm. "Pops, you didn't!"

"Let me see, Mum," said Scratchet, twisting on the spot to get a better view.

"What have you got there, Flotsima?" Nana craned her neck, trying to see.

"I can't believe you did that, Pops!" Mum shouted.

"DID WHAT?!" me, Scratchet and Dad all yelled back in unison.

Mum unrolled the scroll fully in her hands.

"IT'S SANTA'S GREAT DELIVERY MAP!" she howled. "YOU NINKUMPOOPER, POPS!"

Everybody gasped – even Nana Pilchard.

"I couldn't help it," Old Wimbles replied, feebly holding up his palms like Mum was pointing a water pistol at him. "I just saw it there on the front shelf of the big sleigh and I liked the way it twinkled. Nana got to keep Santa's goggles, so I thought I might just keep a souvenir from our journey. Y'know ...

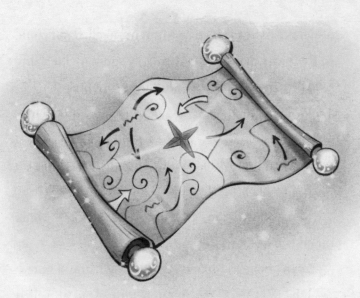

to remember the factory by and all that heartswilly stuff."

"But Santa won't know where he's going without this!" Mum continued to wail. "You might have actually ruined Christmas!"

"Nah," Old Wimbles said, not looking completely convinced. "Santa's done the run so many times, he'll know it like the back of his boots. I'm sure he only keeps the map because it looks all goodsy and glamourly for the big day."

"You'd better hope you're right," Mum said, sternly.

"Well…" Scratchet carefully took the map from Mum and examined it. "Since we've got it, I think we could use a little help in getting to Ingerland."

"Honkswallop!" Nana replied. "Balderdonk! I know, just where—"

"Oh no, Nana," Dad said, cutting the grumpsome elf short. He was leaning over Scratchet's shoulder and examining the map with her. "We *ARE* in India. This is us, see?"

Nana Pilchard didn't turn around, but I think I saw smoke wisping from out of her ears.

Now, this was the first time I had ever seen Santa's legendary map, my human reader, and I'm a three hundred and seventy-six year old Christmas elf … so I'm willing to bet you've definitely not seen it before, or possibly even heard of it. I'll explain how it works…

The Great Delivery Map was created hundreds and hundreds of years ago by mountain trolls as a gift for Nikolaus, the very first Santa. It's drawn on parchment made from the skin of Arctic Hanklebeasts and is enchanted with a spell that can tell you where absolutely anything is. There is a red-and-gold star that marks the exact place where you are in the world, and if you ask it to show you an address, or a place, or a person's whereabouts – *PIFF! PAFF! POOF!* – it'll show you.

"Right, Nana," Scratchet said, sounding very pleased with herself. "Are you ready to follow my directions? I think I can figure this out."

Nana's shoulders twitched, but she didn't say a word.

"Good," Scratchet went on. I was so impressed with how bossy and brave she could be when she wanted to. I wished I could be a bit more like that. "First things first, Nana, we need to turn left and head for Europe."

"BLISTER!" Nana called to the rapidly dashing reindeer without a second glance behind her. "TURN RIGHT, MY FLOPSY FLYER! TURN ALL THE WAY RIGHT! RIGHT, YOU GO!" And with that, Blitzen turned left and we made our way towards Ingerland and our new life in Greymarsh Tower, Trudgeworth.

# Chapter 12

## Greymarsh Tower

"It's not quite what I imagined..." Dad said, screwing up his face and examining the building before us.

By the time we'd found Ingerland and followed the Great Delivery Map to the little town of Trudgeworth, it was already night-time and we were all cold, hungry and exhausted.

Nana had steered poor Blitzen up and down and over and under until she almost refused to fly any more. But luckily for us, after crossing Londish Town for the third time, Old Wimbles and Dad managed to figure out which ways were north and south, and we made it to Trudgeworth for certain.

"Where are the fountains?" Nana huffed. "I expected a welcoming party with little trays of nibblies."

We were standing in a large gravelly courtyard with sleighs-on-big-rubber-wheels parked in rows.

"Human sleighs!" Scratchet said. "There's loads of them."

"They're called carps ... and this is what humans call 'a carp ark'," Dad read from the map as new arrows and words appeared and danced across the surface of the parchment.

"A CARP ARK!?" Nana cooed. "It's all so exotic!"

"But where are all the palaces, Dad?" I asked, eyeing Graymarsh Tower like it had told us a lie. This was all extremely brain-boggling.

"And the music?" Scratchet joined in.

"And all the happy dancing and feasting?" I said. "It is Christmas here, right? I can't even see any twinkly lights or candles..."

"Of course it's Christmas, Gristle!" Dad laughed nervously. I could tell he was worried too.

"I'm sure … I'm sure all the happy human festivities are just happening *inside* Greymarsh Tower. They're waiting for us, my dunklings," Mum stammered. "What should we do, Jiblius?"

My dad jumped at hearing his name and gave a worried squeak, before straightening up and trying to look like he was most definitely in charge.

"Leave this to me, my loves," he said, wedging his hands against his hips and looking around. "I will just … erm… ah, yes… I shall ask him…" Dad pointed to a man who was sitting on a low wall a little way off.

"A human!" Mum gasped.

We all turned with wide eyes to examine what would be our very first elf-to-person encounter. It's hard to believe that we'd all spent our entire lives working to make human Christmases as magical as possible and yet we'd never met one in the wild until this night. I felt the hairs on the back of my neck stand on end and my stomach performed a perfect backflip.

"Don't make any sudden moves, Jiblius," Old

Wimbles advised as Dad shuffled off across the carp ark to speak with … with … agh! It was too bizarre and exciting … and scary…

"Try to act people-ish!" Nana Pilchard barked at the back of his head.

"Good morrow, my festive friend." Dad gleefully beamed as he approached the human, making sure not to make any jerky actions and provoke him. We weren't used to worldly ways after all. "I bring happy greetings from the great Christmas North."

The human looked up and gawped at Dad. "Are you talking to me?" he asked.

"Why, yes! Of course." Dad took a bow and opened his arms wide in a gesture of peace. "Are we in the presence of the fabled Greymarsh Tower?"

The human glanced up at the stark concrete building that loomed above us, then back to Dad.

"Yeah," was all he said.

There was a moment of awkward silence, until…

"Did you do that?" The human pointed to our dumpster that sat at a wonky angle on the completely crushed roof of one of the human carps.

Dad grimaced at the damage Nana Pilchard's landing had caused and tried to look innocent.

"Erm … no…" he fibbed, which was extremely unusual for him.

"That's my Uncle Trevor's car and he's gonna be fumin' when he sees it," the human said. "That was his favourite."

"Worry not!" Dad whooped, trying his hardest to look jangly and joyful. "No one can be fu … fume… fumish, was it?"

"Fumin'," the human corrected Dad.

"Fumin' – I've learned a new word. How marvellous!" Dad hit the human man with one of his best smiles. "No one can be … fumin' … at Christmas time. Now, can you point us to the frivolities, good sir?"

The human frowned at Dad, then smirked. "Why are you dressed like that?" he asked.

"Like this?" Dad showed off his patchwork waistcoat with thimble buttons that Mum had made for his last birthday. "This is my best-best-BESTEST jerkin, and I'm glad you noticed—"

"You look really stupid…"

From our position a little way across the carp ark, Nana huffed. "What did that rapscalliump just say?" she snapped. "Rudesy rumplet!"

Scratchet tried to repeat what the human had called Dad, but Nana didn't wait for her reply.

"Does your mumsy know you talk to people like that, you rottly little rambunker?" Nana marched across the gravel, rolling up her sleeves, while me, Mum, Old Wimbles and Scratchet skittered along behind her.

"What?" the human grunted as he spotted the rest of us emerging from across the carp ark.

"I said, 'Does your mumsy know you talk to people like that, you rottly … little … rambunker?'" Nana said the last words extra slowly for dramatic effect.

"What are you?" the human asked blankly. I could see from this close up that he was actually quite young. What you people-types call a teeny-ager.

"The nerve!" Nana puffed out her cheeks and folded her arms. "I'll have you know, young man, I am … we are…"

160

Dad gave Nana a glance that said "*DON'T TELL HIM WE'RE ELVES!*"

"We are … erm … hu-hu-humans…" Nana said. EVERYONE WAS FIBBING TODAY! "Regulish, humanly folklies doing peoplish thingies."

"You're so short…"

To be fair, the human had a good point. Until now, I'd never realized how much taller you people-types are when compared to us elves. You're twice the size of us. Nana wasn't having any of it, however.

"SHORT!?" she scoffed. "I'm extremely tall actually! I'm just very far away."

"But you're right here," the human was starting to look increasingly flummoxed.

"No, I'm not, you ninkumpooper!" Nana snarled back at him. She jabbed a stubby finger towards the far side of the carp ark. "I'm over there, see?"

The human opened his mouth, closed his mouth, then opened it again.

"I'm just very far away," Nana repeated herself sternly. "And if I was closer, I'd give you a proper tellin' off for saying our Jiblius looks stupid! You're not too old to be sent to your beddy-bunks, mind."

I admit I'd never seen a human before this night, but it was fascinating to watch his face twitch and blush as he tried to figure out if Nana Pilchard was being serious.

"Is … is that a reindeer?" he stammered, nodding at Blitzen who was snuffling about, looking for food between the carps.

"Don't be redunkulous! It's a … umm … it's a mirage…"

"It looks like a reindeer…"

"What's your name, youngling?" said Nana, changing the subject.

"Erm … Greg," the human mumbled. "Greg Bottley."

"That's a stupidsy name," Old Wimbles snickered.

"Don't you start, Pops," Nana growled as she glared at her husband. She turned back to Greg-the-human. "Well, Greg… We're looking for the Pinkerton's home? It's somewhere in that great big block of rock. Do you know it?"

Greg said nothing…

"Don't make me come over there, Gregsy," Nana teased. "I'm nearly ten feet tall and stronger than a barrel-bonker!"

"Eleventh floor," Greg blurted, looking more and more like he might cry at any second. "They live next door to my nan."

"See, it wasn't so difficultsy to be nice, was it?"

Greg shook his head.

"Now BOG OFF before I boot you up the bum-rumps!"

Quicker than an Arctic lemming dashing into its burrow, Greg-the-human leapt over the low wall he'd been sitting on and sprinted away towards a row of brightly lit shops.

"That's how you make enquirelies, Jiblius," Nana chuckled, brushing the palms of her hands together like she was getting rid of dust. "Shall we?"

"Eleventh floor," Scratchet thought out loud. "Maya Pinkerton, Eleventh Floor, Greymarsh Tower, Trudgeworth."

And with that, my human reader, we gathered our belongings, grabbed Blitzen before she chewed another mirror off the side of another carp, and went inside to begin our new human life...

# Chapter 13

## Home Sweet Home

"This is getting a bit blunking boring," Nana grumbled as she banged loudly at one of the doors on the eleventh floor. "I can feel a right stroppler coming on."

My eyes darted towards my nana and I tried not to let a smile creep across my lips. She looked like someone had dragged her through a bramble patch backwards after we'd climbed the stairs all the way from the ground floor. Her flying goggles were askew, strands of flyaway hair were dangling all over her wrinkled face and there were tiny bobbles of fluff sticking to her forehead where she'd wiped her cardigan sleeve across it. The fact that she was also leading a wonky-antlered reindeer along behind her completed her utterly bafflish appearance perfectly.

"Ugh, I'm rantled!" she griped.

Me and Dad had tried to tempt everyone into the metal up-and-down machine when we were downstairs, but the rest of my family all refused.

"I'm not gettin' in that tin bucket cage!" Old Wimbles had jabbered when Dad pointed it out.

"It's a lift," Dad said. "It says so on there, look."

"On where?" asked Nana.

Dad pointed to the button on the wall next to the contraption and read the words that were branded across it: "Call lift."

"Call who a lift?" Nana said, frowning. She turned to Old Wimbles. "You're a lift!"

We'd watched quietly from around a corner, trying to keep Blitzen out of sight, as people came and went from the lift in the entrance hall. A woman stepped inside, pressed a button, and through a little window in the lift door, we saw the whole thing go up. Moments later, it came back down and a totally different woman and her human-child in a wheelie-buggy-thingy got out. It was AMAZING!

"It ain't natural!" Nana Pilchard had huffed. "Going up and down in a box like that. What am I? A doll at Santa's factory? No thank you, sirree, I'm not heaving my bumly-bits into that thing – and neither's Blister, are you my beauty-toot?"

So, there we were, my human reader. All completely frazzled and frizzlied, but we'd finally finished the sweatsy slog up a staircase that smelled like the stables back at the Christmas Factory, and made it to the eleventh floor. The only problem now was that none of us knew which human home belonged to Maya Pinkerton, and there were loads and loads and LOADS!

"Only one way to find out," Nana said after lots of chatter, and she knocked on the nearest door.

"Mother, what are you doing?" Mum fretted as we all waited in silence to see if anyone came to answer it. "We shouldn't draw attention to ourselves."

"It's simple," Nana explained. "We knock on every door we find, and if someone's home, it's not the right one. Do I have to do all the thinkin' around here, Flotsima?"

Mum bit her tongue and said nothing.

"I thought so," Nana Pilchard chuckled. "Now we wait…"

The sound of footsteps could suddenly be heard approaching from the other side of the door and it swung open.

"Hello? Sorry I had the telly on … wasn't sure I heard anythi—"

"Nope!" Nana barked at the startled-looking woman inside the door. "Wrong one!"

"Is … that a real reindeer? Are you carol singers?" the lady asked, eyeing the extremely short frump-dumpling of a bedraggled granny standing before her.

"Who are you calling 'Carol'?" Nana juffed at the woman. "Blunkin' cheek!"

"Oh … sorry … erm … can I help you?"

"You already have, thank you, madam," Nana replied after a moment of travel-weary glowering.

She forced an unconvincing smile, then curtseyed. "Now, trundle off and enjoy your din-dins."

Without another word, Nana walked to the next door and banged again – harder, this time. A man wearing an apron and oven gloves answered.

"Yes?" he said. "Ah, carol singers."

"Oh, bumlies to her," is all Nana moaned at him, before grunting and skuddling off down the hall. "Blinkin' Carol. Onwards!"

Twelve doors and a lot of startled residents later, Nana knocked on another door and waited, still grumbling to herself about *Carol*.

"Yes?" an old lady answered and peered around the edge of the doorframe. "Is that you, Greg, dear?"

*Greg?* At least she hadn't asked after *Carol*, I thought...

Nana opened her mouth to let out what I could imagine was going to be a long line of rude words that Christmas elves should definitely not be saying, and so I stepped in front of her before she had the chance.

"I'm terribly sorry ... erm ... Mrs Bottley?" I said,

desperately hoping I'd got her name correct. It was just a hunch. "I got the wrong door."

The old lady blinked at me through her thick spectacles and smiled.

"Not to worry, little fella," she rasped.

Phew! I was right.

"Happens all the time in this place. Everything looks the same after a while, doesn't it?"

"I know, Mrs Bottley," I chuckled, trying my hardest to seem calm and confident. "Well, enjoy your evening."

"You too, ducky."

With that, the human lady closed her door and we listened to the sound of her feet shuffling away. I turned around to see my family all gawping at me like I had just grown a tail.

"What?" I asked, feeling my cheeks flushing pink.

"You never told us!" Mum sighed. She rushed towards me and flung her arms around my neck. "Oh, Gristle, how lovelish."

"Told you what?"

"Your elf-magic is improving!" Mum said, almost

on the brink of tears. "I'm so proud of you!"

"Mum, I have no idea what you're talking about," I muttered.

"You're psychic, Gris," Scratchet grinned, nodding with approval. "That's a handy gift to have."

"I'm not psychic…"

"Yes, you are," Scratchet replied. "You knew that old lady's name… I'm impressed."

"No, you bunch of nonk-plonks!" I laughed. "Have you forgotten already?"

"Forgotten what?" Nana croaked irritably.

"Greg Bottley!"

"Who's Greg Bottley?" wheezed Old Wimbles.

"Greg Bottley!" I repeated, rolling my eyes as my family stared blankly back at me. "The human teeny-ager in the carp ark downstairs."

"Oh, him," said Mum with a shrug. "What about him?"

"He said his Nan lived in Greymarsh Tower … and that old lady asked for Greg after we knocked on the door."

"Is that so?" Dad said. "I was so excited about

seeing humans in their own habitat, I barely listened to a word the boy said."

"And there's more…" I announced, feeling a spark of joy ignite in my belly. "He said his nan lives next to—"

"A polar bear?" my grandmother interrupted.

"No, Nana!"

"A big rock?"

"No!"

"How many words?" Nana asked. "Act out the first word… I'll get it! Is it a book or one of those moving picture thingies?"

"Nana, this isn't a guessing game," I humphed. "Greg Bottley said his nan lives next door to Maya Pinkerton."

"Oh, that," said Nana flatly. "I knew that!"

Ignoring my nana's prattle, I turned to the next door along the hallway and…

"That's it!" I gasped. The next door was painted a deep blue colour and there were cheerful stickers in the shape of letters stuck to it.

"Maya lives here," Mum read aloud, tracing her

finger along the name that had been spelled out. For a second it looked like she might have a little cry. "We actually found it."

Everybody went silent and we all stared at the closed front door of our new home. This was it, my human reader. We had made it all the way to Trudgeworth, Ingerland from the North Pole, and now our very own human Christmas experience was about to begin. Who knew what wonders were on the other side of this door? I closed my eyes and saw mountains of gifts just for us, mince pie platters, music and singing, and absolutely no stress or worry ever again.

"Get this thing open will you, Scratchet?" Nana Pilchard whispered loudly behind her hand. "I'd ask Gristle, but his elf-magic isn't improving after all."

Scratchet smirked at me, then lifted her hand to the keyhole, closed her eyes and wiggled her fingers.

*CLINK! CLICK! CLACK!*

It sounded as if some invisible person was picking the lock. Scratchet really was a marvel at these sorts of things. She scrunched up her face in concentration.

"Come on," she mumbled to herself. "Where's the latch?"

*CLUNK!*

"Got it!" Scratchet cooed. "That was a tricky one. Human locks are really different to the ones on the barn door back ho—" She stopped herself mid-sentence, and we all felt a little pang of sadness for the life we'd left behind us.

"That ain't our home any more, Humbugs," Nana Pilchard said. "There's no use gripin' and snizz-grizzlin'. We've got to remember those blunkers at the factory didn't want us. We're not just stable stubs any more and we have a squibbly new home to enjoy. I name this palace HUMBUG HALL!"

And with that, Nana barged the door open with her hip, took a deep breath and led the way into our new life.

# Chapter 14

## Settling In

*I* don't know what to tell you, my human reader. Just walking into Maya Pinkerton's home felt like we'd discovered Christmas for the very first time, after hundreds and hundreds of years toiling, trying to make other people's Christmases special. It was wonderful!

Before you could shout *THIS IS HONKHUMPTIOUS!* we were tearing through the rooms, exploring the nooks and crannies and having a proper holly-day hullabaloo.

I admit HUMBUG HALL wasn't exactly the ... what was it again? ... the Taj Mahal. There were no white marble staircases or fountains or ballrooms or peacocks strutting across manicured gardens, but this little place was still a thousand times nicer than the Humbug hayloft back at the stables. It wasn't draughty or smelly and the floor was covered in the most incredible fluff-grass to keep your tootsies warm. There was even a mat on the floor with the word WELCOME written across it. Maybe Maya Pinkerton knew we were coming after all?

"AAAAGH!?" Nana Pilchard cried from one of the rooms. "I CAN'T BELIEVE IT!" She'd gone ahead to check the place was safe, and now everyone raced in to see what she was screaming about.

Only moments before that, we'd all been standing in a long room that extended away from the front door, marvelling at the rows of hooks on one side with lots of coats and bags hanging from it.

"Are ... are they for us?" Mum stammered. "Gifts?"

"Of course. I think you just take whichever one you like," Dad said. "I bet Maya Pinkerton left them there especially."

"I can have any of them!?" Mum's voice was quiet and trembly. "I've had the same coat for five hundred years."

"Take your pick, dunkling," Dad said. "Don't forget, we're living as humans now.'

It was around that moment that Nana had hollered, and we all (except Mum) ran through, only to find ourselves in a room covered in cupboards with a table and chairs at the centre. Nana was slumped against the door of a tall white box that hummed quietly to itself in the corner.

"What is it, my sweetling?" Old Wimbles asked, doddering to his wife's aid.

"Be still, my tunkerous heart!" Nana warbled. She looked like she'd just had the fright of her life.

"Oh, Nana!" Scratchet yelped. "Are you all right? Have you seen something dreadful?"

"MY EYES!" Nana screamed. "MY EYES!"

"Oh, baubles, what's happened?" Mum followed

us into the room, wearing a bright yellow coat with a smiley-faced raindrop on the front. "Mother?"

"Flotsima, is that you?" Nana croaked feebly. She held her little hand out in front of her like she couldn't see.

"Cripes! What's going on?" Mum looked panic-stricken.

"It's in here," Nana wailed.

"Is it terrible?" asked Dad. "I don't want to look!"

"You have to see, Jiblius," Nana blubbed. "You have to!" She twisted on the spot and flung the white-hummy-box door open as she screamed with wild abandon.

In no time, we were all screaming alongside her.

I have no idea if you have one of these contraptions in your human home, my human reader, so I'll tell you all about it.

Nana yanked open the door and a light filled the room that made us all squint. *Who keeps light in a box?* I remember thinking, *That's a stuperous place to keep light!* but it wasn't the light that my grandmother was wailing at.

As my elf eyes adjusted, I saw ... I saw ... the box was cold inside and had little shelves filled with ... with – I have tears in my eyes just thinking about it – the shelves were filled with FOOD!

"IT'S A FEAST!" Dad roared, and he wasn't wrong. Inside that tall-coldy-box-thing we found a pot with something called yogurt inside it. There was a piece of ham! We unscrewed a jar of pickles and another filled with sweet and bitter gloop called Marmy-lade. "I've never seen so much food!"

"THERE'S MORE!" Old Wimbles started opening all the cupboards and pulling out crinkly bags of crispies, a slightly mouldy loaf of bread, and squeezy bottles filled with red sauce called klup-chup.

"Look at this!" Scratchet whooped. She'd climbed on to the counter and was busily turning a metal valve attached to a pipe that poked out of the countertop. We all watched as a stream of water came from the end of it and splashed into the sink below. "It comes out hot and cold depending on where you twist this little handle! AMAZEROUS!"

"Boogle my bunions!" Old Wimbles spluttered, his mouth full of crispies. "It's a feasting bath! A FEASTING BATH! These humans know how to live, by jingles!"

He quickly dragged a chair across the floor and wedged it up against the low cupboards. I swear I'd never seen the raggedy old groaner move so fast in the last two hundred years.

"This shindig is just getting started," he laughed.

In a matter of seconds, Old Wimbles was completely

nudesy, sitting with his bumly-bits in the basin of warm water, merrily singing, and shovelling fistful after happy fistful of snacks into his grinning gobblet.

"BLISSLY!"

While Old Wimbles soaked and snacked, the rest of us explored Humbug Hall, chattering and skipping about as we went.

There were two rooms with great big beds in them and lots more clothes in the wardrobes. In one of the rooms, the clothes were made to fit a much bigger adult human, but there was lots we could wear in Maya Pinkerton's room. We knew it was hers because her name was on the door in more of those little letter stickers.

"I don't ever want to move again," Mum chuckled as she flopped on to the bed and kicked her legs this way and that. "It's much nicer than a hammock made from hay sacks."

In another room, we found more of those twisty handles that made water pour from pipes, and even rain from the ceiling!

"What does this do?" Dad thought out loud as he pressed a silver button on top of a low half-seat/half-basin thing. There was a loud *WHOOSH* of water and we watched as it flushed into the bowl and then disappeared.

"There are fountains after all!" hooted Dad.

"I think that's a poodly hole," Scratchet snickered. "It's where humans go for a … you know…"

"How strange!" Dad said with a smile. "What's wrong with flinging it off the roof?"

"We're humans now, Jiblius," Mum corrected Dad, looking a little bit flustered. "We've got to behave all proper and nicely from now on."

A little further down the corridor, we found the biggest and weirdest room of Humbug Hall. It had a huge comfy-squishy-seat in the middle that seemed to point towards a big black rectangle on the wall and there was a … well … there was a sort of … umm … tree in the corner.

"What in the blunkers have they got a shrub-a-dub inside for?" Nana said, scratching her chin as she stared at the odd thing. "That's not where they live. Do you suppose it's lost?"

Scratchet reached out and touched one of its branches.

"It's not real," she said. "And there are little beads on strings wrapped around it."

"Don't be redunkulous, Scratchet," barked Nana. "Who would bring a pretend tree indoors and then give it jewellery? These human-types are weirdsier than I thought."

"I mean it, Nana," Scratchet went on. "They lead

to…" My sister's voice trailed off as she followed the string of beads to a white square on the wall. "There's a switch on it," she said, and gave the thing a click.

Instantly, the string of beads wrapped around the not-a-real-tree sparkled with coloured lights and the room was illuminated with a festive glow.

"Oh, my dunklings," Mum said. "How beauty-bump."

"It looks like the lights inside the toy workshops," I mumbled, feeling a tiny jolt of sadness. I clenched my toes and tried not to think of the North Pole.

"It's perfect," Dad sighed, pulling us all into a hug. "This is going to be the best really-real Christmas we've ever h—"

*CLUNK! CLICK!*

It was the sound of a key in the front door.

Light from the outside hallway spilled across the long coat-room and we all instinctively dived behind the huge comfy-squishy-chair.

"Don't be long, sweetheart." A gravelly man's voice spoke, although we couldn't see him from our hiding-place in the not-a-real-tree room. "Your gran will have dinner on the table soon and you know how she gets if we're late."

"I won't, Grandad," came another much younger voice and I watched, peeking over a plump cushion, as a young human girl walked down the long coat-room towards us.

"That must be Maya Pinkerton," Scratchet whispered to me and I felt a tingle of exhilaration crackle up my spine.

We'd already glimpsed a small handful of humans since arriving in Trudgeworth, but this was completely different. Maya Pinkerton was the reason we were here. If we hadn't found this little girl's letter, we would never have gone to the Big House, Scratchet would never have dinged the emergency donger, Bungustus McMerrypie would never have spotted mince pie crumbs on my blanket-coat, we would never have been banished to the frozen white waste or stolen Blitzen, or broken in to our new Christmas home.

"That's weird," Maya Pinkerton said, stopping at the not-a-real-tree room door.

"What is it, darling?" the voice of Maya's grandad asked from the front door.

"The Christmas tree lights are on," she replied. "Mum never leaves them lit when she's at work."

"Can you switch them off?" The man's voice asked. "There's a good girl."

Maya Pinkerton walked into the room and I saw her in full for the first time. She was wearing blue trousers, a red-and-green striped top and had shoes that flashed with lights when she walked.

"I want me some magic shoes like that," Nana muttered from behind the comfy-squishy-chair. "I wonder if those are beef wellingtons?"

"Shhhh, Mother!" Mum hissed quietly.

"I bet they're warm and juicy…"

Maya Pinkerton vanished behind the not-a-real-tree and the lights on a string clicked off, plunging the room into darkness, except for the glow from the corridor. She was just backing her way out when she called to her grandad again.

"Grandad, there's a pickle behind the tree with … I think it's been dipped in yogurt and marmalade!"

186

"Oh, crumbles, that was mine," Scratchet murmured.

"Hurry up, love," Maya's grandad called from the hall. "Your gran is texting. Dinner's almost ready. Grab what you need and we'll get going."

"All right," Maya Pinkerton replied, but I could tell she was suspicious. She dropped the half-eaten pickle into a little bin by the bookcase, then looked around the room like she was searching for secrets. "Hmmmm."

With that, the human girl turned and walked out of the not-a-real-tree room and headed into her bedroom instead. Less than a minute later, she emerged again with some clothes tucked under her arm and a book in her hand.

"Are you all done?" her grandad asked.

"Almost," Maya Pinkerton called back.

She disappeared from view for a second and everyone got a bit twitchy, to say the least.

"Oh, baubles," Mum fussed in almost silence.

"What's wrong?" Dad asked.

"There's a nakesome old elf taking a bath in the

food-room water bowl and a reindeer eating greens from the tall-coldy-box-thing!"

"Oh, grump-lumps, I'd forgotten about Pops," Nana gasped.

"Please don't go in the food room," Mum pleaded with … I don't know … the universe? "Please don't go in the food room."

"Are you ready, Maya?" her grandad called one last time.

"Yep!" Maya Pinkerton replied. "She emerged from the rainy-poodly-room, carrying a little bag full of washing-type-thingies. By some Christmas miracle she hadn't gone into the food room and hadn't had the scare of a lifetime. No one in the world deserves to unexpectedly stumble upon nudesy Old Wimbles, that's for certain.

"Don't forget your raincoat," Maya's grandad called. "It's going to pelt it down tomorrow."

My throat dried out and I thought I could see stars when Maya Pinkerton stopped at the coat hooks and examined the garments for a second.

"Grandad," she said.

"Hmm?"

"My coat's not here – it's gone."

"Oh, no … oh, no … OH, NO!" Mum worried as quietly as she could from our hiding-place. She was wearing a fetching new raincoat that she'd nabbed from the hooks.

"Nothing to fuss over," Maya's grandad said. "It must be in your rucksack back at ours. Now come on, we've got to get moving."

Maya Pinkerton stopped in front of the not-a-real-tree room doorway one last time and peered in. I could tell she knew something wasn't right.

"Oh, and don't forget that book you're reading," Maya's grandad called one last time. "Your mum wanted you to bring it with you."

Maya Pinkerton glanced down at the book in her hands, thought for a second, then placed it silently on the low table in front of the comfy-squishy-chair.

"Don't worry, Grandad. I won't forget it."

And with that, she left…

# Chapter 15

## Outside...

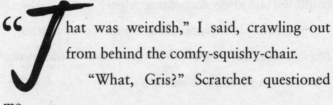

"That was weirdish," I said, crawling out from behind the comfy-squishy-chair.

"What, Gris?" Scratchet questioned me.

"Maya Pinkerton's grandad asked her to remember to bring her book..."

"Yeah?"

"And then she said she wouldn't forget it."

"Yeah?"

"And then she put it on the table and left anyway."

I couldn't put my finger on what was going on, but something seemed slightly odd about the whole thing. "I think—"

"Don't care," Nana Pilchard groaned as she clambered back to her feet. "That human girl might live here with her nurse-mumsy, but she's bogged-off now and I want more CHRISTMAS in my holly-day home!"

"What do you want to do?" Mum asked. "I feel all giddy and free. We could play games, or tell stories?"

"Nah!" Nanna blurted. She placed her fists on to her hips and doddered over to the not-a-real-tree room window. "This is all very nice and all, but I think we need something a bit more raucously and festified. We've missed out on so many Christmases, my Humbugs, and it's time to really enjoy ourselves. My clunkered old hearty wants to party!"

"What are you plotting, Mother?" Mum asked cautiously.

"Nothing," Nana muttered unconvincingly. "That looks like fun, though."

She nodded to something out the window and we

all hurried over to see what Nana was referring to.

"I like all the lights and busy peoples." Nana Pilchard beamed. "I bet it would be hootsy to go out and meet the neighbours. Imagine how many gifts they'd give us! That's all humans do! Everyone knows it!"

We all reached the window and looked down to see what my ancient grandmother was talking about.

The view from the eleventh floor of Greymarsh Tower was really something, my human reader. We could see for miles and miles over the rooftops of Trudgeworth from up here. There were lights twinkling everywhere and fine snowflakes had started to fall from the blackening sky.

"I've never seen so many buildings," Dad wheezed in surprise.

"Look down there," Nana instructed us all.

We glanced at a town square a little way off from our new tower home. There were rows of little shops on two sides and then a great big shop in the middle. It was enormous! Even bigger than the sleighworks and the Great Letter Hall combined. Outside, in the centre of the town square, we could see a pine tree covered in lights, just like the one right here in Maya Pinkerton's home, only much larger, and there were rows of people singing carols around it.

"That's where ... what was his name? Greg? That's where Greg Bottley ran off to earlier," Scratchet said, steaming up the glass with her breath.

"It looks like fun to me," Nana cooed. "Let's go!"

"Hold your humplets, Mother," Mum said. "We can't forget that we're elves, and we've broken into someone's empty home, and we shouldn't attract any more unwanted attention or we could end up being rumpscallions in both the elf world and the human world."

"That would be dreadful," Dad said, shaking his head.

"That would be exciting," Nana Pilchard cackled.

"Mother!"

"Oh, stop your worrying, Flotsima. I'm just kiddling with you. This place is full of stuff and junklies. A few disguises will keep us safe to enjoy the festivibles."

"Oooh! Disguises!" Scratchet cheered. "Now that sounds like fun."

"Right you are, my dunkling." Nana patted Scratchet on her head. "Now let's get changed. We'll all be little incognetoads hopping about."

"I don't know why I had to wear this," Old Wimbles grumbled as we crossed the patch of dead grass between Greymarsh Tower and the shopping precinct. He was already in a mood because Nana had dragged him away from his feasting bath, and now she'd forced him into a flowery dressing-gown that had been hanging on the back of the rainy-poodly room door, then pulled all the feathers out of one of the cushions on the comfy-squishy-chair and wedged the empty cushion cover on to his head like a floppy nightcap, he was even moodsier.

"I think we look brilliump," Mum sighed, looking at each of us one by one.

Dad cut a hole in the not-a-real-tree room rug, stuck his head through and was wearing it as a flashy and fuzzy cape; Mum was zipped up tight in Maya

Pinkerton's yellow raincoat with a blue woolly hat pulled down over her pointy ears; Scratchet was wearing practically everything she'd found in the wardrobe all at once; I had wrapped my head in a scarf and bundled a blanket around my shoulders; and Nana Pilchard had stolen the knitted thing she'd found on the teapot in the kitchen and stuck it right the way down over her head with her face poking out of a hole on the side.

"We look just like one of these humans," Nana said confidently as we reached the edge of the square. "No one will suspect a thingly, I promise it."

"I hope so," replied Dad. He spotted a man and a woman heading in our direction from across the square and waved politely. "Good evening, human! I mean, people-types. Lovelish night for a stroll in my favourite rug, what, what?"

The couple gawked at Dad, then us and hurried past, laughing and gossiping to one another.

"Hmmm, I don't know how well my human impression is working?" he said with a worried look on his face. "Maybe I'm not getting the words quite right?"

"Gobbledygunk!" Nana snapped at Dad as she started marching out across the square. "You're doing it perfect, Jiblius. Those snobblies only rushed away because they'd never seen such humanish humans before and it made them feel slopsy about themselves."

"Oh, right." Dad gave an embarrassed grin. "That's all fine, then."

"'Course it is. We're blendin' right in."

We all followed Nana Pilchard as she marched past the carol singers around the tree and headed for the big shop straight ahead of us.

"Those aren't the words!" she bellowed over the singing as the poor people tried to get through a rendition of … well … the humans were singing "While Shepherds Watched their Flocks by Night", but every elf knows it's really "While Santa Darns his Socks by Night". "You're doing it all wrong!"

Sometimes I don't think Nana Pilchard understands what blending-in really means, my human reader. All the singers got very jittery about the tiny angry lady with a teapot hat on her head. One of the men singing extremely loudly on the front row, reached the high note at the end of the song and accidentally spat his false teeth out across the cobbles!

Anyway ... as I was saying ... Nana led the way across the square, making a straight line for ... I read the vast neon sign out loud: "Bargain Land: Everything you'll ever want in one handy superstore".

"Oooh, it sounds so exciting," Mum beamed. "I can't believe we're actually going to experience our first human Christmas. We're going to get gifts!"

"What's a bargain?" asked Scratchet.

"Sort of like a dolphin," Nana instructed her with perfect confidence. "But more bar-y and definitely a lot more gainy."

"WOWZERS!"

"Everything you'll ever want," Old Wimbles cooed as he re-read the shop sign while passing beneath it. "I want a bath ... on wheels ... with an oven for pastries."

"They'll EASILY have that," Nana Pilchard laughed. "You're not thinking big enough, my lambly."

She stepped up to the enormous doors and just like that, as if they'd been expecting us, they glided open all by themselves, displaying rows upon rows upon rows of Christmas gifts, books, clothes, toys, food, bicycles, gadgets and gizmos, and all of it was for the taking.

"Come on, my lumplings," Nana cheered like she was marching off to battle. "We're not in the North Pole now. Let's go get our grabbers on some Christmas swag."

# Chapter 16

## And So, This Is Christmas ... Isn't It?

"*I* ... I never knew there were so many things in the world," Mum blubbed as we walked into Bargain Land, dressed in our finest human disguises.

"And it's all for us," Nana Pilchard sighed. "D'you know, I could get used to being a person-type, I could. They lead a life of lovelishness. Fill your pockets, my dunklings. We're not elves any more and EVERYTHING IS FREE!"

It didn't take us long to start tearing up and

down the aisles of that place, grabbing at anything we wanted. I don't quite know how to describe the feeling, my human reader, although I'm sure you've felt it too, being a person and all.

When you've grown up having nothing, being able to have anything you want makes your skin prickle and your brain fizz. Suddenly you can't live without any of it.

Me and Scratchet grabbed one of the pushy-wheely-carts and headed along the first row of shelves with greedy peepers and busy hands.

"Definitely one of these," Scratchet said as she grabbed at some kind of spice grinder, slinging it absent-mindedly into our wheely-cart. "And five of these!"

We seized at mops and bananas, clothes and cooking pans, perfume smellies and rolls of tissues for flushing down the poodly hole. Scratchet took armfuls of little towels for washing your face and I scooped up a whole stack of plant pots.

"It's amazerous to think we can just take all this stuff." Scratchet laughed. "Why did we stay at the North Pole for so long? Human lives are THE BEST!"

We pushed our wheely-cart up and down, occasionally spotting our family as we went by.

Nana Pilchard was in the clothing department, swishing in circles, wearing a gold sparkly dress that was probably twenty sizes too big for her. She twirled and pirouetted, admiring herself in a nearby mirror.

"Looking great, Nana!" Scratchet called. Nana Pilchard turned to us and struck a fancy pose with one hand in the air.

"I feel like Mrs Claus. Haha!" she guffawed. "This is HUMDIFFEROUS!"

Further around the enormous shop, after heaving two telly-boxes and a pair of roller skates into our wheely-cart, we saw Mum in the book aisle, blushing as she read the latest romance novel by a big famous writer I'd never heard of.

"I didn't know words like this existed!" she huffed, looking a little sweaty. "You haven't seen your father, have you?"

Just by chance we had seen Dad, one aisle earlier.

He'd kicked off his worker boots and was sitting on the edge of a large freezer, dangling his wriggly-toed feet among the packs of frozen peas and eating an ice-cream cone.

"This will do wonders for my aching trotters," he said, smiling dreamily. "What a dreamish new life, eh, Gris?"

"It's brimly, Dad," I replied, but the truth is, I was feeling a little strange. All around us were busy humans, getting their last-minute shopping before the big day, but nobody seemed ... well ... very Christmassy.

For instance, most of the humans we encountered looked more frazzled and frowny than festive, and when me and Scratchet were wandering up the food aisles, I saw two men arguing over a pack of Brussels sprouts.

"Move!" another lady barked at us as she tore along a row of shelves looking for something she obviously couldn't do without.

"Everyone's a bit grumpus," I mumbled to my sister when we rounded the corner. "Look!" I pointed to a red-faced man in a suit who was yelling at another man behind a counter filled with meats.

"I'm sorry, sir, we just don't have any larger turkeys left," the worker-man said from behind the counter. "They've all been bought."

"Well, it's just not good enough!" the other human hollered. "GO AND FIND ME ONE NOW!"

"I promise this is the biggest one we have left." The shop-worker looked exhausted and about as far from Christmassy as anyone could get.

"IDIOT!" the red-faced man bellowed and stormed off to some other part of the shop.

"That poor person," I muttered, looking at the dejected worker-human.

"We all know how he feels," Scratchet shrugged.

"Can you do something?" I asked her. "With your magic, I mean."

"What like, Gris?" my sister moaned. "There's more stuff to grab and we haven't seen some of the aisles yet."

"Just a little something ... to cheer him up," I pleaded. "Anything?"

Scratchet thought for a moment, and then a look of mischief crept across her face. I knew she wouldn't be able to resist the challenge of performing elf-magic.

"All right ... but quickly!" She giggled, before pointing to a stack of Christmas cards on a nearby shelf. "Grab one of those..."

I did as Scratchet had asked and before long we were huddled together, staring down at the blank inside page.

"What shall we say?" she asked.

"Umm..."

"Never mind," she said impatiently, scrunching up her eyes and wiggling her fingers. "I've got this. Something uplifting, I think, and a little bit soppsy."

Before our eyes, loopy writing started to curl its way across the white paper. "*You're Brilliumtious!*" it said. "*The world is better because you're in it. Merry Christmas!*"

"There! That should do the trick," Scratchet said, smiling. "Is that slobberchopsy enough for you?"

"It's perfect, Sis," I replied. "You're so good at that."

"Good? I'm astoundabus! Watch this…"

As if carried by an unexpected wind, the little Christmas card suddenly jerked out of Scratchet's hand and flew in a perfectly straight line towards the man at the meat counter. Just when it looked like it was going to hit the glass at the front of it, the card twizzled upwards and landed right in front of him, next to where the knife and chopping board were placed.

"Don't let him notice us," I gasped as he spotted the little red envelope and looked about for its owner, so we ducked back around the corner we'd just come from.

"What's he doing?" Scratchet snickered, enjoying the sneakiness.

I peeked between two large boxes of caramel chunklets and saw the worker-man open the card and read it, before a smile … a really-real smile … illuminated his face.

"Hmmm." I sighed happily. "That made everything feel better."

Watching a worker in this huge magical shop

instantly reminded me of our life in the stables. "I wish someone had given us a card and told us the world was better because we were in it occasionally."

"Yeah, yeah, yeah," Scratchet replied, sounding less than interested. "But do you want to know what can brighten your evening even further?"

I turned to my sister and saw that she was practically trembling with excitement and yet more mischief.

"What?" I asked, slightly nervous about the reply.

She pointed upwards and I followed with my eyes. There, hanging over our heads was a sign that said *NEXT AISLE: CHRISTMAS CAKES, PUDDINGS AND MINCE PIES.*

# Chapter 17

## Double Crumb-inals!

"Jump on, Gris!"

Scratchet pushed the wheely-cart so quickly around the corner to the next aisle, I had to grip on to its side with all my strength.

We swerved past a mountainous stack of jars filled with sticky pickle, nearly flattening a human lady and her two squabbling children in the process, and emerged around the corner into a wonderland of pastry proportions.

"Pinch me," Scratchet huffed as we juddered to a

halt, staring at the rows and rows of crumbly mince-filled masterpieces that stretched away from us on either side. "I'm not dreaming, am I?"

"It's real..." I gurgled. "M-mince pie p-p-paradise!" My mouth had stopped working as it hung greedily open, and I wasn't entirely sure, but I thought I could hear an orchestra playing.

There were boxes and boxes of the delicious pies in endless lines, and in the middle of the chequered floor, sitting cross-legged between the two unending shelves, surrounded by torn cardboard and crumpled-up foil tart cases, sat...

"Pops!" Scratchet called. "You started without us."

It seemed Old Wimbles had found this irresistible aisle before we had and we'd interrupted him having a gobblunctious feast for one.

"Kiddywinkles!" my grandpops cheered, firing crumbs of mince pie in all directions. He tore open another box and beamed at us. "Come and join me; there are squillions of 'em, look!"

Abandoning our wheely-cart piled high with

gifts we'd grabbed for ourselves, me and Scratchet bounded over to join our grandpops. It's hard to describe the feeling of elation that rippled through my elvish bones at that moment, my human reader. Here we were in your world, living like you humans, eating mince pies in the middle of a giant shopping aisle just like you humans do.

Admittedly these mince pies weren't nearly as good as the ones lovingly created in the bake house back home, but *OOOOH* they were still good enough and I was ready to fill my face.

We deserved it, didn't we? The Humbugs had all spent so much time living and breathing Christmas at Santa's factory, but never actually enjoying it … never taking part. It was like hearing the most beautiful song in the world, but only from very far away where the notes get jumbled and you can't quite tell what the words are saying.

But not any more. Now was our chance to relish this magical time of year. Now was our chance to be spoiled for a change and to feel as festive as a workshop elf. NOW was our chance to—

"Oi!" The voice was gravelly and angry, and it certainly didn't seem to go with my perfect fantasy Christmas that was unfolding all around me. "What d'you think you're doing?"

We froze on the spot with half-eaten mince pies hanging out of giddyishly greedy gobs.

"STAY RIGHT WHERE YOU ARE!" Another equally angry voice roared.

At the end of the aisle, humpling towards us like a pair of menacing walruses, were two humans dressed in uniforms.

"Don't take another bite!" one of them threatened as he balled his boiled-ham hands into fists.

"Thought you'd have a little picnic, did you?" the other leered. She was even bigger than her meatish friend. "We've seen this type of 'smash and scoff' before."

"Don't get all noggin-bothered, my big bunglies," Old Wimbles said with a mince-smeared grin. He tore open yet another box of pies and held one up as a peace offering. "There's plenty to go around. Here you go, friends."

As the humans clomped closer, I could see the badges on the front of their uniforms read: *BARGAIN LAND SECURITY TEAM*.

"They're guards, Grandpops," I whispered as visions of the workshop brutes swam across my memory. Something about this pair and their scowly-frowns told me they weren't happy that we were eating the mince pies.

"Nonsense," Old Wimbles chuckled. There's nothing to guard in a snackly place like this, Gris. You eat anything you like. Everyone knows that." He took another chomp of pie. "See? Plenty for all of us."

"Sir," the lady-guard growled, "I won't warn you again. Put the pie down and slowly stand up."

"If it's all the same to you, dearie, I think I'll stay on my rumples while I'm eatin'. I get a bit gutsy if I snaffle standin' up," Old Wimbles said, nodding politely and patting his tummy. "You're welcome to join us down 'ere though."

"Pops," Scratchet mumbled, dropping the empty crust that she'd been nibbling. "I don't think the nice lady wants us to eat any more."

"Haha!" Old Wimbles was refusing to listen, as usual. Ancient elves could never be told anything. "Where'd you get an idea like that, young'un? It's Christmas! Join me, friends, one and all." He tossed a mince pie into the air, opened his mouth as wide as he could, then caught the entire thing in a single huge gulp on the way back down. "Delunktious!" he squelched with a faceful of food.

"That's it," the lady-guard snarled. She reached down and dragged Old Wimbles to his feet. "Don't say I didn't warn you, sir."

"Bleurgh!" Old Wimbles spat the remaining pieces of pie out, looking more startled than a reindeer on a rollercoaster. "What's the meaning of this? Unhand me, you bargious bully!"

"There'll be none of that!" boiled-ham hands joined in with his partner, grabbing me and Scratchet by the backs of our necks. "Is this your trolley?" he asked us, nodding to the wheely-cart crammed to bursting with all sorts of brilliant Christmas gifts.

"Yes," Scratchet replied. "We got all the best stuff, I think."

"I presume you are planning to pay for all that?" the man-guard croaked.

"OF COURSE NOT!" Scratchet burst out giggling. "That's a good one, Mr Guard-man. You're funny!"

"Eh?"

"It's Christmas," Scratchet went on, hopefully. "You don't pay for things. It's all free and made with love!"

"Get 'em out of here," the lady-guard bellowed, before the three of us were dragged, wailing and flailing, back towards the entrance of the store.

"You'll go on the naughty list for this," Old Wimbles threatened as he thrashed about. "It's coal for you next year!"

As we were paraded through Bargain Land, I noticed more and more people peering around corners or pausing their conversations to stare at us. People started pointing and laughing, and some of them took photo-thingies on their little phone-squares.

"Don't you jabbergiggle at us!" Old Wimbles

hollered at a group of teeny-agers, who were jeering and making fun. I spotted Greg Bottley amongst them.

We passed a row of funny bleep machines where humans were scanning their goods and putting them into bags, and as we got nearer to the front doors of the almighty shop, I could hear more yelling and kerfuffling.

"Nana!" Scratchet yelped.

I looked up and saw another burly security guard hauling Nana Pilchard towards the exit from a different part of the store.

"I'm about to CLUNGDUNGLE you right in the bonce if you don't put me down!"

Nana was wearing about ten different sparkly dresses, one on top of the other, with so many necklaces and bracelets she was jangling like Santa's sleigh.

"Get every single fashion item off now!" her guard demanded. "AND MAKE IT QUICK!"

Nana wriggled and squirmed her way out of all the twinkly clothing, then dumped it on the floor at her stubby feet.

"Me own rags are much more comfortous anyway, you big meat-monger!" Nana shouted. "Who d'you think you are, ruining my Christmas dress-up?"

Before the guard had time to answer my ferocious nana, another lady rounded the nearest aisle, dragging Mum and Dad behind her.

"I found these two trying to clamber over the cheese counter," she said, shoving Mum and Dad towards us.

"There was glass in the way," Dad tried to explain. "We couldn't go through it, could we? We had to try and climb over or we wouldn't be able to reach the cheese!"

"That's not the point," the guard grunted.

I looked around at my slightly bedraggled family and we all formed a group right there on the enormous Bargain Land doormat.

"You can't do this at Christmas," Old Wimbles huffed, shaking his fist at the gaggle of security guards. "It ain't festive!"

"You'll be straight on that list," warned Nana Pilchard.

"I already told 'em that," Old Wimbles blurted to his wife. "Told 'em clear as day. You'll all get lumps of coal next year when Santa hears about this."

"Pah!" one of the guards laughed at us. "And what are you? Santa's little helpers?"

"That's right," Dad said. "We *ARE* Christmas

elves and it would seem that you've all forgotten about good cheer and ... umm ... merriment ... and..."

"You're fooling no one, you little weirdos," the lady who'd dragged Mum and Dad sneered. "Christmas elves? What a load of old rubbish!"

"Codswallop!" guffawed another.

"Just a load of stupid stories."

The words hit each of us like stinging pins. I felt dizzy and strange. The floor seemed to be moving about beneath my feet and there was a pain in my stomach like I'd been kicked.

*Rubbish?* Did they just say *codswallop? Stories?*

Nana Pilchard reeled backwards and grabbed my wrist to steady herself. She looked up at me with large frightened eyes.

"We have to go," was all she wheezed...

# Chapter 18

## Close Encounters
## of the Maya Kind

"Rudesy little rumplets!" Nana growled. We were back at Humbug Hall and my nana's shock had turned into red-hot fury. She was pacing back and forth in the not-a-real-tree room like a little unexploded volcano.

"Who do they think they are, calling Christmas 'CONKSNOT'!?"

"I think it was '*codswallop*'," Scratchet muttered.

"I KNOW WHAT THEY SAID!"

"Calm down, Mother," Mum said quietly.

"CALM DOWN!" Nana booted a cushion that had fallen off the comfy-squishy-chair across the room. "I've never been so insulterated."

"I think we could all use a cup of tea," Mum thought out loud. "I wonder if Maya Pinkerton has any in the food-room?"

Suddenly the strings of lights on the not-a-real-tree sparkled to life and Dad backed out from behind it.

"There," he said with a feeble smile. "That makes everything feel a bit more festiverous, doesn't it?"

We all nodded quietly. Nobody looked very festiverous right now.

"Look, I'm sure they didn't mean..." Mum attempted to cheer us up, but she gave up mid-sentence.

"Of course they didn't mean it," Dad joined her. "Those guards were just trying to judder us. It's their job to be all tough and mean. That's all ... I hope."

"So, is this Christmas?" The words came out of my mouth before I had even thought to say them. "Is this it? All that we've been looking forward to?

We've worked our whole lives ... not just us ... every elf at the factory has worked and worked because it made Christmas lovelish for the humans, and after all this time, they ... they..." I couldn't say it, it was too heartbreaking.

"They don't care about Christmas!" Scratchet said it for me.

"Worse than that," Old Wimbles grumbled, looking extremely uncomfortable on the comfy-squishy-chair. Blitzen had wandered in when we arrived home and was now flopped over my grandpop's lap, snoring peacefully to herself. "They said Christmas was just a load of stories. Those block-bonced bunglers don't even believe in us! 'Ere, watch your horns, Blister, you nearly took my eye out!"

"How could they not believe in Christmas?" Mum snuffled. "That's impossible!"

"It's just a lot of greedy grabbing and face-stuffing," Scratchet whimpered. "I feel a bit sick."

"We were told it was all about love and gifting and friendly fussing," Old Wimbles barked over everybody else. "But it's actually just a load of ME-

ME-ME! My Great-Uncle Grumple was right. Never trust Southerners."

"All the humans were so grouchous in the big shop," I continued, feeling tears welling-up at the corners of my eyes. "They were fighting and snatching and being unkind to each other. Pops might be right … except for the Southerners bit … that's just silly."

"I always am," Old Wimbles looked pleased with himself, then remembered what he was correct about and frowned instead. "And it ain't silly, Gristle. Watch your language."

"Maybe only the moodsy ones were out this evening." Mum tried to comfort us. "That's it! We only saw the moodsy humans with no Christmas cheer. We've all heard the scary stories about such people existing, haven't we? I bet all the cheery ones are at home, snuggling with their families, waiting for Santa to arrive."

"It has to be true," Dad agreed.

"Think … erm … think of Maya Pinkerton and all the other children who wrote letters to Santa," said Mum. I could practically hear the thoughts bouncing around inside her head. "They believe, don't they? They wouldn't have written if they didn't think Christmas was real."

"I suppose," Scratchet mumbled. "I thought tonight would be a lot more smiley and not quite so pointy and laughy. Maybe we—"

*CLUNK! CLICK!*

The sound of keys in the front door made us all jolt with fear. We spun around to face the not-a-real-tree room door as a light from the outside hallway filled the long coat-room and the shadow of a young human child crossed the floor.

I barely had time to even think about hiding when Maya Pinkerton sprinted into view.

There was a moment of complete bewildered silence as she stared at us, a family of Christmas elves lolloping about her home, and we stared right back.

It was only when Blitzen sprang clumsily off the comfy-squishy-chair to get a good sniff of the stranger who'd just wandered into Humbug Hall that chaos broke loose.

Maya's face contorted in terror as the huge

antlered beast bounded towards her. She let rip with an ear-ringing scream, and in turn, we all howled right back at her. Mum and Dad leapt into each other's arms, Nana toppled backwards and sprawled across the fluff-grass floor, Old Wimbles buried his head beneath a pile of cushions, Scratchet curled up into a ball, and I just stood and watched in stunned stillness as Maya turned and ran into the rainy-poodly room, slamming the door behind her.

# Chapter 19

## Maya Pinkerton

"Maybe she's dead in there?" Old Wimbles mused.

"Oh, stop it, Pops!" Mum snapped at the clunkery old elf. "You're not helping."

"She might be!"

"STOP IT!" Mum turned back to the rainy-poodly room door and knocked gently. It had been over an hour since Maya Pinkerton had arrived home unexpectedly and locked herself away in shock and fear at seeing a family of elves and a slobbering reindeer in her home. Mum knocked again. "Maya, it's all right. We're not going to hurt you."

"Try this," Nana Pilchard said from behind us. She reached between me and Dad, handing Mum a ... a...

"What's that?" Mum asked, wrinkling up her face.

"Pig stick," Nana said flatly.

We all stared at the strange snack in Nana's hand. It was one of those sausagish things I'd seen in the old recipe book.

"Found it in the food room," Nana went on. "Humans love pig sticks. She'll be right out here, snuffling and snorting in no time, she will."

Mum tried knocking again.

"Maya, you can come out, dearie. We're all very friendly."

"I'm not," Old Wimbles blurted. "Not all the time."

"Shut up, Pops!" Mum mouthed the words at him, before she turned back to the door. "We'd love to meet you, Maya, and we've got a ... umm ... pig stick..."

There was a gentle click and the rainy-poodly room door opened a smidgen. An eye peeked out at us.

"Haha! Nana knows best," Nana Pilchard chuckled. "Pig stick wins!"

Maya stared at us for a moment of silence.

"Who are you?" she finally whispered.

"Oh," Mum straightened herself up and smiled sweetly. "Hello, Maya Pinkerton, we're the Humbugs."

There was another silence as Maya stared. I could see her looking us up and down.

"Come and join us for some porky pig stick, dearie!" Nana coaxed the human girl.

"I don't like sausages, sorry," Maya replied nervously. "I'm vegetarian."

"And I'm Nana Pilchard," my nana said with a smile. "Now we're not strangers."

"I would never have guessed that Maya was short for Vegetarian," Old Wimbles muttered to himself. "That's not an obvious one."

"How do you know my name?" asked Maya.

"Oh, that's easy," beamed Mum. She turned

to me and pulled a face, as if to say *"tell her what happened"*.

"Maya," I said, stepping forward so she could see me through the crack in the door. "Hello! My name is Gristle and I'm … well, I'm a Christmas elf."

The door flew open and Maya appeared in full view, she was holding the poodly-hole brush like a weapon.

"You're fibbing!" she gasped.

"No," I replied. "Christmas elves never lie."

"I do," Old Wimbles added behind us, but everyone ignored him.

"How did you get here?"

"We flew," I said. "You already met Blitzen. Sorry if she scared you."

"Blitzen is a girl?"

"Yep," Scratchet answered. "All the best ones are."

"Mum's not going to be pleased there's a reindeer in the living room."

"Oh, is that what you call it?" Dad said.

"I don't suppose we need to tell her, if..." Maya really stared at each of us, one by one. "You're not lying, are you? You really are Christmas elves?"

"We really are," I replied.

"I KNEW IT!" Maya Pinkerton forgot her fear in an instant. She dropped the poodly-hole brush and took a big step towards us. "Earlier when my grandad brought me over to get my stuff, I could tell someone had been in the flat. I just felt it. Mum never leaves the tree lights on and I thought I heard someone whispering about beef wellingtons."

We all looked at Nana Pilchard, who just shrugged back at us.

"That was Jiblius," she said.

"No, it wasn't," Dad shot back.

"Fibster!" Nana pointed a finger at Dad. "He's been jabbering on about beefy boots for as long as I can remember."

"Mother, you're not fooling anyone!" Mum said in her sternest voice.

"Fine," Nana griped, folding her arms in defeat. "So, I may have talked a little bit about 'em. I just fancied a warmly present, is all."

"You're early for presents this year," Maya went on. "It's not Christmas Eve for another two days."

"Isn't it?" Nana said. "D'you know in all the upy-downy-runny-rushy-ness of the recent goings-on, I'd clean forgotten what day it was."

"But…" Maya looked confused. "You're elves. You have to know what day Christmas Eve is." She looked over our shoulders expectantly. "Is Santa here? I'd love to meet him. I drew a picture for Mrs Claus and everything!"

"Ah, you see, Maya," I muttered, not wanting to disappoint her, "we're not here to deliver you Christmas presents, I'm afraid."

"Why have you come then?" she asked. "I sent a letter to Santa because I'm going to be at Gran and Grandad's. I thought that's why you're here early…"

"It might be a good idea to sit around the table and have a cup of tea together," Nana Pilchard suggested. "Tea always helps, I think."

"Mum only drinks coffee," Maya replied. "I could make some squash, though."

"I don't know about that, young lady," Nana grumbled. "Sounds painful and I barely know you."

Maya giggled, then took Nana Pilchard's hand.

"It's not that kind of squash," she said. "This way…"

# Chapter 20

## A Little Bit Right
## and a Little Bit Wrong

"*Y*ou left the North Pole?" Maya gasped. We were all sitting around the table in the food room, enjoying a squibbly-tasting drink of *squash*. It turns out this strange human drink is only a kind of fruit cordial made from oranges, despite its worrying name.

"We did," Mum said. "We all left together."

"Oh, I'd love to visit Santa's factory. I bet it's the happiest place in the world."

I caught Scratchet's eye from across the table and she grimaced at me. We may have come to Trudgeworth and Greymarsh Tower to get away from all the unfair treatment and rottlish living conditions at the factory, but I certainly didn't want to ruin this little girl's dream of what it was like.

"Bits of it are," Mum replied.

"That's putting it generously," Nana grumbled under her breath.

"Only bits of it?" Maya asked, licking her lips where a halo of bright orange squash had settled. "I thought it would be brilliant in every part! I've got a book in my…" Maya reached down to where she'd dumped her rucksack by her feet and fished out a beautifully illustrated children's book called *Santa's Little Helpers*. "Here, I borrowed it from school. It's for little kids, but I love it. I borrow it every year for the holidays."

She pushed the book across the table towards Nana, who took the thing in her hands like it was a trick and about to go *POP!*

"I really love books," Maya cooed with a grin. "I

left another one of my school books here on purpose when I went off to Gran and Grandad's house earlier. That way I'd have an excuse to come back here after dinner and see what was going on."

"I spotted you doing that," I chuckled.

"Me too! Very sneaky," Scratchet joined in. "You're my kind of human, Maya Pinkerton."

"I just felt sure that if I came back, I'd see Santa." Maya said. "It was a tingly feeling. I've been trying to spot him for years. I suppose a family of Christmas elves is almost the same. Better in fact!"

"Don't your gran and grandad mind you wandering back here alone?" Mum asked, looking concerned.

"No," Maya replied, smiling. "They live right there by the big shop."

"BARGAIN LAND!" Dad yelped way too enthusiastically.

"That's right," Maya said. "They're not far, and as long as I only cross the big square that's always busy with people, they don't mind."

"Guh!"

A grunt from across the table distracted us from our conversation and we all turned to look at Nana Pilchard. She was thumbing her way through the picture book and was somewhere between laughing and crying about it.

"Would you look at this!" she squawked. "I can't believe my peepers!"

Nana held up the open book and showed everyone a great big picture across two pages of Santa's workshop. There were happy elves skipping and dancing about while Santa was painting a toy train in the middle of the drawing.

"It's lovely, isn't it?" said Maya.

"It's WRONG!" Nana barked back at her. She puffed out her chest and fought off a very unfestive scowl.

"What do you mean?" Maya asked.

"This book's all completely clunkered! Santa doesn't do any work, the lazy lumpus!" She jabbed a finger at the rosy-cheeked fellow in the illustration. "That plonkle hasn't done a day's work in yonks and yonkers. Painting a train indeed!"

"Oh," Maya looked a little worried.

"And get a look at this jibberwonk!" Nana carried on griping as she turned the page. We all looked to see a drawing of the stables and ... well ... my jaw hung open with surprise, my human reader. Is that what people thought life at the Christmas Factory was like?

There, in the picture, were dozens and dozens of crisply dressed elves, all happy and beamish, tending to the most pristine and brightly lit stable you could ever imagine. Reindeers pranced, everything was neatly swept and there was absolutely no...

"WHERE'S ALL THE POO?" Old Wimbles blurted. "Where are the holes in the roof and the icy draughts and squidgerous floors? Why don't any of those whoppsy-brained elves look exhausterous or back-breakish?"

"There aren't any of those things," Maya giggled. "Life in the North Pole isn't like..." She stared at us for a moment. "Is that what it's like?"

It was Mum who decided to break the awkward silence.

"Listen, Maya, my dunkling. Sometimes, what we're told about a place isn't always entirely true."

"Is it horrible there?" Maya looked utterly shocked.

"No, it's not horrible," Mum replied. "A lot of it's wonderful. But ... it's not all skippy and laughy for elves like us."

"Elves like you?"

"We weren't born into poshly families," Nana Pilchard said, tossing the picture book over her shoulder. "If you ain't a high-and-flying tra-la-la type, you're a worker elf ... and that means lots of drudge-budging and not nearly as much thanks from those lazy lot who lord it about above you."

"That's why we came here." Scratchet leaned in and gave Maya's hand a squeeze. "To Greymarsh Tower. Ever since we were all young lumplings, every elf in the North Pole has shared stories about the human world and how HONKHUMPTIOUS it is. There are famous songs about the amazerous feasts and all the gifts you peoplish-lot receive at Christmas, and we decided to come and see for ourselves."

"Like a holiday?" said Maya.

"Almost," Mum winced a reply. "We were sort of thrown out of the factory. It's a long story, but Nana Pilchard biffed the workshop boss."

Maya gasped.

"He deserved it," Nana moaned to herself. "And the rest of 'em."

"But," Mum went on with forced cheerfulness, "coming here was an easy choice to make when the alternative was turning into elfcicles in the frozen white waste."

"Why did you choose my home though?" Maya cheered, clapping her hands. "Did I win a competition or something?"

"No!" Scratchet whooped. "We found your letter!" She plunged her hand into the top pocket of her jerkin and whipped out Maya's yellow envelope. "Look! It got lost in the snow and we saved it. We were heroes for five minutes. That's how we knew your address."

Everyone watched as Maya's face fell and a look of sadness swooshed across it.

"So, Santa doesn't have my letter?"

"No. It's just ... erm ... well, I think..." Scratchet mumbled. She itched her head and frowned. "I ... I didn't think of that..."

"Oh, Maya, I'm sorry," I said as reality hit me like a mince pie in the noggin. How in all this time had it not dawned on us that we hadn't actually handed Maya Pinkerton's letter over to Santa? I swear I'd never felt so muck-dumpy in my whole life, my human reader.

"Santa doesn't know where to deliver my notebook and pens?"

"Oh, sweetling," Mum blubbed as she realized too. "Because of us, Santa doesn't even know what you wanted in the first place."

Silence fell over the little room and we all stared at the table-top for what seemed like an eternity. Had any elves ever committed such a terrible crime? I couldn't imagine they had. It's one thing when Christmas post goes missing, but quite another when Christmas elves actually stop a child's note from getting to the Great Letter Hall. We had ruined

Maya Pinkerton's entire festive season. We deserved to be thrown out into the frozen whi—

"It's all right," Maya said quietly, making us all look up and gawp at her.

"What's that?" Nana Pilchard huffed, cupping her hand around her ear. "Say it again?"

"It doesn't matter that I'll be left off Santa's list this year." Maya nodded and looked content. "If it means I get to meet you all instead."

"B-but ... your present," Dad stammered.

"I don't mind," the little girl said. "I never get much at Christmas anyway... I was going to give this present away, so it's all fine really."

"What are you talking about, littl'un?" Old Wimbles wheezed. "Don't you get showered with gifts and snacklies, surrounded by big honkerous parties and such?"

"No." Maya laughed. "No, nothing like that. I think we've both been told the wrong things about where the other half lives."

"But even if you're missing out on Santa's special gift this year, you humans give each other piles of presents, don't you?" Dad asked, looking dumbfounded. "You'll get lots of other things to open on Christmas day?"

"Nope." Maya shrugged. "Mum works super hard at the hospital and we don't have too much money, so we always keep it small and nice. Just us. She says '*It's not about things, it's about people.*'"

"Is that so?" Old Wimbles asked, stroking his beard.

"M-hmm. Mummy thinks family and friends are better than anything that can come wrapped in a box." Maya said. "So I'm not upset about the letter. Don't worry."

Mum looked like she was going to burst into tears. "Your mumsy sounds very—"

"Stupid!" Old Wimbles cut in.

"NO, POPS!" Mum told him off so loudly, my grandpops turned away and flushed the colour of holly berries. "As I was saying, Maya, your mumsy sounds very smart indeed."

"Well, what do you know?" Dad sighed, sipping his squash drink and looking lovingly around the room. "Elves want to be humans, humans want to visit the North Pole; elves make toys for humans, and here we are talking to a little girl who doesn't need toys and just wants her family." He paused for a moment of thought. "Something has gone very wonksy along the way…"

# Chapter 21

## The Lives of Human-Types

*I*t didn't take long for Maya Pinkerton's gran and grandad to call her home in Greymarsh Tower to find out why she was taking so much time collecting her book.

"Sorry, Gran!" she said into the chatty-phone-stick after she plucked it off the wall. "My book is so good, I ... erm ... I started reading it and got carried away."

"Come back now, darling," we could hear Maya's gran saying. "It's getting late. I'll send Grandad out to meet you in the square."

Maya replaced the chatty-phone-stick, turned to us, and her face flashed with a little of Scratchet's mischief for a moment.

"I have to go now," she said. "I'll be back in the morning though. Mummy's working all night tonight, so you'll be safe until ten a.m. tomorrow. You'll have to leave for a few hours when she's here for her breakfast and a shower, but we can go out and have some fun. I'll show you around."

"Oh, that sounds squibbly!" Mum cooed. "I just got a judder of excitement at the thought of exploring around a human town."

"Thank you, Maya," I sighed, handing her the backpack she'd left on the food-room floor. "I'm really sorry about your letter."

"Don't worry, Gristle," she said, giving me a hug around my middle. I didn't say anything, but I may have secretly wept a tear that moment. It was my first ever human hug after all! "Having real elves like you coming to stay is much better than a notebook and pens. I couldn't ask for more."

Maya turned to where Nana Pilchard and Old

Wimbles were rooting through the tall-coldy-box-thing, opening jars and sniffing their contents.

"Goodnight, Humbugs," she called as she headed for the door.

"Dream sweetly, little miss," Old Wimbles called back. "See you in the morning."

I chuckled to myself then, trying to ignore the guilty feeling that bubbled about in my belly. Old

Wimbles really can be charming when he wants to be...

I waited at the not-a-real-tree room window until I saw Maya skitter across the square far below and meet her grandad by the Christmas tree at the centre of it. I don't know why, but after all the miles we had travelled, all the trouble we'd been in, and just how incredibly kind she had been, I felt suddenly protective of Maya Pinkerton, similar to the way I felt about Scratchet.

"Merry Christmas, Gris," my little sister said to me when she spotted how deep in thought I was. I jumped and she smiled at me from the doorway, then tossed me an apple she'd snaffled from the tall-coldy-box. "We did good, you know? Not exactly how we should have done things, but good all the same."

My family spent the rest of the evening huddled together on the comfy-squishy-chair, completely transfixed by the black rectangle shape on the not-a-real-tree room wall. Scratchet had picked up a little gadget with white and red buttons on it from the low table, and when she pressed one of them, the FABULOUS contraption flickered to life.

"EURGH! What is it?" Nana Pilchard yelped when a nature programme appeared on the screen and a lion ran towards us, roaring. "It's a big rat! Make it go away, Gristle!"

With the click of a button, we watched all kinds of bizarre and brilliant things that night. There was Christmas carol singing; funny moving pictures called cartoons (I liked the one about a boy and his flying snow person friend the best); a lady making a big bowl of gloop called a trifle; people making Christmas decorations out of things they'd found in the bin; a game show where people answered questions all about the past year; and a sad film about a giant ship that sank in the ocean with an old lady and a necklace – we were all blubbering like hysterical hyenas at the end.

By the time everyone was ready to go to sleep, no one could quite decide where was best. It was very confusing. After all the fantasizing about a real snuggly bed, we tried out the big one in Maya's mum's room and found it was WAY too comfortable.

"I can't snizzle and snooze on that thing," Old Wimbles grumbled, prodding the soft squidginess of it with a stumpy finger. "It's like a cloud, it is. I need something lumpsome and scratchy if I'm going to drift-off." And he was right…

We'd all spent hundreds of years dozing in tanglish hammocks and discomfort was as normal to us as fluffy sheets are to you, my human reader. So, we finally curled up together on the hard food-room floor, bundled with knobbly-bobbly blankets Mum had brought from home, windows wide open for a frosty draught, and enjoying the gentle and familiar whiff of Blitzen being stinkly in the corner. Who knew, after all this time, we'd need a little bit of the stables to really relax?

"Morning!"

I opened one eye and stared up at the blurry face of Maya Pinkerton.

"There you all are," Maya laughed. "I expected to find you lot in the bed or on the sofa."

"What time is it?" Nana grumbled as she rolled over and blinked her salty eyes widely.

"What day is it?" Old Wimbles groaned. "I dreamed we stole a reindeer and flew around the world."

"You did!" Maya replied. She stepped over me and Dad and bustled into the food room, dumping her rucksack on the counter. "I grabbed us some breakfast from Gran and Grandad's."

"Oooh, what is it?" Nana sat up and rubbed her hands together greedily. "I'm very knowledgous about human food, you see, Maya Pinkerton. I'm an expertle! I know everything. Every single thing you eat, Nana Pilchard has read about it."

"Buttered crumpets," Maya said, grabbing see-through packets of little cake-looking things from her bag.

"Never heard of 'em," Nana humphed and laid back down.

"They're delicious and my grandad has packets and packets of them. He won't notice if a few are missing."

In no time, Maya had clunkered around the food-room and assembled our first ever human breakfast on the table.

"It's all ready," she cooed, ushering us into the chairs. "I wasn't sure what elves like to drink, but Mum always has coffee at breakfast, so I made you a pot."

We watched as Maya dished out the steaming crumpets, two each on to little plates and poured black and strong-smelling liquid into mugs.

"*Bon appétit*," Maya beamed.

"WHAT DID YOU CALL ME!?" Nana gasped. "I've never been so insulted!"

"No, no, no!" Maya looked like she'd just upset a grizzly bear. "*Bon appétit*! It means *good appetite* in French, Mrs Humbug! Mum taught it to me. You say it when you want someone to enjoy their meal."

"Oh." Nana shrugged lazily. "I know ... I thought you said ... erm... bald apple teeth ... and there ain't nobody who's going to call me that before I have my—"

Nana took a slurpy sip of the coffee and froze.

She suddenly had the look of someone who'd just been slapped around the face with a cod fish.

"Do you like it?" Maya asked. "Mum has it every morning. She says it keeps her awake when she's got a long day at work."

"It's ... bleurgh ... it's awful!" Nana griped, pulling a face. She took another sip. "Actually, it's delunktious!" She took yet another sip. "Ugh, it's horrible!" And another sip. "It's like liquid sunshine!"

We easily finished the tummy-tinkling crumpets and ... well ... no one else drank any of the coffee after Nana turned into a jabbering chattersaurus. She polished off five cups of the stuff, coughing and spluttering with disgust and swooning over how tastyfied it was, until she was practically fizzing with energy.

"Let's go!" she hollered, slamming down her empty mug and jumping down from the table. "I want to see the town, the buildings, the people, all of it, LET'S GO! NOW!"

And *GO* we did...

*

Long before Maya's mum got home to shower and nap before running back to work in the hop-spital, our new friend led us out into the hallways of Greymarsh Tower, down the stairs (Nana still refused to take the lift), and out into the carp ark. We tied Blitzen's reins to a low fence behind a nearby hedgerow and left her with a bucket of our nibbled apple cores to keep her busy.

"Nobody ever comes around the back here," Maya reassured Mum, who was getting very worried and twitchy. "Blitzen will be safe for a few hours."

"So, where are we going first?" Nana shouted. She clearly wasn't too fussed about Blitzen being discovered. "This way or that way? Quick! Tell us!"

"What would you like to see first?" Maya asked, trying to keep a straight face.

"You choose," said Dad. "None of us know this town better than you."

"That's right," Mum agreed after a few slow breaths to calm her nerves. "If it's Christmassy, we'd love to see it, Maya. Eee! I can't believe we're going out for festive fun today. If we were back at home, we'd be shovelling more poo than ever! They feed the reindeer double this close to the big day."

"Okey-dokey," Maya cooed. "There are lots of things around town for us to do and see. This way…"

"Won't your gran and grandad wonder where you are?" Mum asked before we set off.

"Stop fussing, Mum," Scratchet groaned. "Maya's a tricky smartling just like me. I can tell. She'll have thought of something, I bet. Didn't you, Maya?"

"I told them I was spending the day with friends," Maya replied over her shoulder, making her way towards the square.

"All right, but you mustn't tell fibs," Mum warned the young girl.

Maya stopped in her tracks and turned to face us Humbugs with a look of complete happiness on her face. "I didn't," she said to Mum. "It's the truth."

# Chapter 22

## Christmas in Trudgeworth

I don't know what to tell you, my human reader. At the risk of sounding incredibly squidgerous and slobberchopsy, we had the most interesting day wandering around Trudgeworth with Maya Pinkerton.

If I'm totally honest, and I feel like I can be with you, I was secretly a little bit disappointed when we arrived here in the human world.

After all the stories of great feasts, and festive dance balls, and avalanches of gifts, and music and laughter filling the air, the sight of Greymarsh Tower with its grey walls, and grey windows, and grey-looking inhabitants, left me feeling less than merry.

It made me miss the lanterns, and the snow, and the Northern Lights above the North Pole.

But while we were out with Maya Pinkerton on the day before Christmas Eve, we discovered a whole different kind of Christmas, the likes of which us elves had never heard of.

Out on the square, even though it was only just after breakfast time, the carol singers were back, rattling buckets and collecting money for something you humans call *charity*. It's a new word to me, but I like it very much.

Again, when I saw the carolers in full daylight, my first reaction was to feel a bit ... I don't know ... let down, I suppose. I'd seen pictures of carol singers on a squillion Christmas cards sent to Santa Claus and hung around the factory on paper chains, but these people didn't look anything like them.

On the cards, carol singers wore big hoopy skirts with shawls and bonnets, or smart tailcoats and top hats. Everyone was neat and pretty, with rosy cheeks and eyes that twinkled by the light of candles they were carrying. But the Trudgeworth Singers were a raggle-taggle bunch, wearing ripped trousers and big puffy coats, singing the wrong words and cracking high notes. None of them seemed particularly energetic, and one lady was eating a sandwich and chewed while she sang!

It was just then, however, that something struck me, my human reader.

These carol singers were just like my family. We didn't look anything like the elves you see on Christmas cards. We weren't always energetic or rosy cheeked, but we still go out and do what we have to in order to bring joy to others. They might not look like the pictures on cards and in books, but Christmas wouldn't be the same without them … or us…

I watched as people came and went from the shops. Some of them looked happy and waved to friends as they passed, but not everybody did… Some people looked downright pooped and exasperated. I could see they were muttering lists to themselves, counting their last pennies in their purses, or sprinting about to make sure they got everything done on time, and – hear me out before you think I've driven my reindeer-pulled dumpster on too many loop-the-loops – I thought they were BRILLIANT!

It never occurred to me before, that the stressed people dashing about town, or grumbling at their kids, or grabbing at things on the shelves in Bargain Land were still doing their bit, pursuing a happy Christmas regardless of how tired, or grumpy, or poor, or stressed, or overworked they felt. These people were keeping the cogs of Christmas turning.

Suddenly the lights, and snow, and mountains of presents that we'd been fooled into believing were the very heart of Christmas seemed very silly indeed … or at least a little meaningless if they don't come along with friends and family to share them with.

Maya took us to the Trudgeworth Christmas market, and just the same as the carol singers, it didn't look anything like we'd been told it should. There were no Alpine lodges selling carved souvenirs, or vats of mulled wine billowing clouds of spiced steam into the air, but there were people nattering and having a giggle with friends and family. It felt like half the town was there, buying crackers to go on their tables and colourful knick-knacks to hang on the tree.

"You wouldn't catch me eatin' one of those," Nana Pilchard huffed when we passed a man selling – I jolted with surprise – HOT DOGS!? "I bet you get fur stuck in your teeth."

"I'd have a nibble," Old Wimbles said, smacking his lips together.

Later, Maya showed us the river and we fed the ducks. We visited a skating pond that was INSIDE! Who knew you humans would do something so strange? An indoor skating pond? Haha!

We stayed for a while, swooshing and spinning, until Old Wimbles tried to out-skate Scratchet, fell on his rumpus and had an almighty tantrum about it.

"Ruined!" he wailed from the middle of the ice. "My bumly-bits are RUINED, and so is Christmas!"

It was only when we were crossing the square again, on our way to get baked potatoes (Maya insisted they were yummalicious with beans and cheese, and her grandad had given her some money to spend), that we heard a voice calling from the direction of Greymarsh Tower.

We all turned to see a lady who looked just like Maya, striding towards us.

"I thought that was you, darling," the lady said, waving.

"Mum!" Maya ran and flung her arms around the lady's middle.

"What are you up to?" Mrs Pinkerton asked. "I thought you were at Gran and Grandad's."

"I'm just showing my friends around the market," Maya said, looking back towards us. "We're going to get baked tatties."

Mrs Pinkerton glanced our way and her eyebrows raised with polite shock.

"And who are your friends?" she said through a gritted-teeth smile.

"This is..." Maya pointed at Scratchet. "Sally,"

she said, before pointing at me. "And this is Gr … Graham. They both go to my school."

"Oh." Mrs Pinkerton looked at us suspiciously. "I've never seen you in Maya's class before."

"They're exchange students from … erm…"

"France!" Mum blurted.

"Bulgium!" Nana Pilchard cut-in at the same time. She took Mrs Pinkerton's hand and shook it vigorously. "I'm their grandmoo and this is the rest of the family." She gestured grandly towards Mum, Dad and Old Wimbles. Everyone grinned back nervously.

"Well, it's nice to meet you, Mrs…"

"*Bon Apéttit!*" Nana Pilchard exclaimed. "Mrs Bon Apéttit. It means *shut up and eat your grub* … or something. Very French, it is. French-Bulgium-ish."

"I promised I'd show them what a Trudgeworth Christmas looks like," Maya said, distracting attention away from Nana.

"That's kind, darling," Mrs Pinkerton said, before planting a kiss on her daughter's head. "Ugh, I miss you."

"Are you going back to work?" Maya asked.

"Yes." Mrs Pinkerton nodded, and it was just then I noticed how tired she looked. "It's another all-nighter. Things are terribly busy and there's still not enough staff."

"You poor lumpling," Nana Pilchard cooed. "Have they got you running about like headless chungles at that hop-spital?"

"I'm afraid so," Mrs Pinkerton replied, stifling a yawn. "Do you mean *hospital*?"

"Mum saves people's lives every day," Maya announced proudly. "She makes poorly people well again."

"A hero!" Old Wimbles whooped.

"Oh, it's not quite that dramatic," Mrs Pinkerton said. She looked embarrassed and stared at her feet.

"People like you must be so fussed over," said Mum. "What a valuable member of the town."

Mrs Pinkerton rolled her eyes.

"If only," she sighed. "Endless work and not a lot of thanks for it."

"Like us!" Scratchet gasped.

"What's that … erm … Sally?" Maya's mum asked.

"Nothing," Scratchet replied, then pretended she didn't understand the question.

"Right, well, I have to get moving," Mrs Pinkerton groaned. "Have fun with your friends, darling, and don't forget to check in with Gran and Grandad, will you?"

"I promise," Maya said, and with that, her mum turned and hurried off across the square.

Evening arrived, and after joining in with the carol singing, trying our first custard doughnuts, and watching a cartoon about a witch who had lots of animals on her broom, Maya had to return to her gran and grandad's house.

"It's nearly dinner time and they'll be expecting me soon," she said, clambering off the comfy-squishy-chair.

"I wish you could stay," Scratchet moaned. "I haven't even told you about flying over the Taj Mahal yet."

"You can tomorrow," Maya said, grinning as she grabbed her rucksack from the hall. "It'll finally be

Christmas Eve. That's the best day of the whole year for telling stories."

"Bye, Maya," Mum called from the food-room.

"Bye, Humbugs!" Maya called to everyone as she waved from the door. "Bye, Gristle!"

I admit, my human reader that I'd been deep in thought ever since we'd got back that afternoon and had barely heard Maya as she was getting up to leave.

"Gristle, I said bye!"

"Oi, boogle-bonce!" Scratchet cooed with a giggle. She tossed the telly-box button-gadget at me. "Earth to boogle-bonce!"

I glanced up and was surprised to see Maya wrapped in her coat and scarf, ready to return to her gran and grandad's house.

"Oh, are you off?" I asked. "I ... I was thinking ... umm..."

"Where have you been?" Scratchet snickered at me. "You look like you were miles away, Gris."

"I was," I replied.

"What's wrong?" Maya walked back into the

room towards us with a look of concern. "Have you not enjoyed today, Gristle? I'm sorry…"

"No, no, it's nothing like that," I said, still trying to sift my way through the sloshy feelings in my head. "I had a wonderfus time … it's just…"

"Just what?" Maya asked.

"I keep thinking about your poor mum, having to work all over Christmas."

"Don't worry, Gristle, she does it all the time," Maya said, with a smile and a shrug. "This is normal to us."

I nodded, but something about that made me feel all wrong and wonksy. I couldn't get the thought of Maya's Christmas letter out of my mind. Christmas gifts didn't matter to her… I'd already figured that out. The best present of all would be for Maya's mum to be around.

"What's going on inside that noggin' of yours?" Scratchet teased. She poked me in the ribs. "You look like you're about to burst into song."

"Worker-humans…" I muttered.

"Huh?"

"Worker-humans are just like us worker-elves …

they deserve a bit of extra love on the special day."

"You've got that right," Scratchet agreed. "If they're missing Christmas, it's a shame—"

"It's a shame Christmas can't come to them..." I finished my little sister's sentence as an idea fizzed across my thoughts. "Your mum can't be here, but there's no reason we couldn't send a little magic her way instead, is there?"

"What do you mean?" Maya mumbled, with a mixture of excitement and worry.

"Maya," I said, feeling my skin tingling, "can you take us to your mum's hop-spital?"

Maya's face fell with disappointment.

"I think it's too late," she sighed. "The hospital is right on the other side of town and by the time we've walked there, I'll be late for Gran and Grandad. They'll be furious!"

It was just then that my brilliump sister caught up with my plan and jumped three steps further ahead, just like she always does.

"Who says we have to walk?" Scratchet smirked with a twinkle of imp in her eye.

# Chapter 23

## Magic... Sort of...

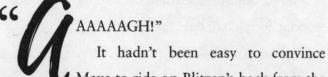

"AAAAAGH!"

It hadn't been easy to convince Maya to ride on Blitzen's back from the dizzying heights of the eleventh floor, but somehow, we'd managed it with the promise of spreading a little Christmas magic.

"You're clear for take-off," Nana Pilchard announced as she flung open the not-a-real-tree room windows, letting in a heavy gust of snow-speckled wind.

"I'm not sure about this," Dad said, stroking his moustache. He always did that when he was anxious.

"Oh, don't spoil their fun, Jiblius," Nana scoffed, pulling the curtains to one side. "Now, hold on tight, my lumplies, and remember old Blister's a bit of a wonk-rocket."

It was all a total blur, my human reader. After ordering the absent-minded reindeer NOT to fly, Blitzen wobbled her way across the room, still chewing on one of Maya's mum's slippers and ... it's hard to find the right words ... just ... sort of ... flopped out into the night air like she was simply toppling into a hay bale for a nap.

"AAAAAAGH!"

Maya was sitting at the front of the saddle, desperately clutching on to Blitzen's antlers, with Scratchet behind her, and me at the back, as we instantly found ourselves plummeting down the side of Greymarch Tower with all the grace of a horned sofa that had been thrown off the roof.

"Make it fly!" Maya screamed. "Make it fly!"

My head felt like the inside of the mixing vats

back at the North Pole bake house. I tried to steady my vision, but the whole town was spinning around us and I wasn't sure if Blitzen had even realized we were outside free-falling towards the ground. She showed no sign of attempting to save us or even herself as we tumbled and spun.

"We're going to DIIIIEEEE!" Maya bawled. "We're going to—"

It was Scratchet who finally managed to scream an order to the oafsome creature before it was too late.

"DOWN!" she screeched. "DOWN, BLITZEN! GO!"

In a flash, our reindeer steed stopped in mid-air and hung there casually, still chewing on the slipper, while the three of us on her back heaved an enormous collective grunt.

"Guh!" was all Maya managed after a second of gobswonkled silence. "I think I'm going to be sick."

"Is it over?" I whimpered, daring to open one eye. I peeked downwards and saw we were hovering just above the carps in the carp ark. "Are we dead?"

"Not yet, we're not. That was fun!" hooted Scratchet.

"Fun!?" Maya stammered with the voice of someone who ... well ... who'd just fallen out of a tower block on the back of a brainless beast. "That was the worst ... the worst..." She thought for a second, and took a deep breath. "THAT WAS AMAZING! I'M ON A FLYING REINDEER! I wish my friends at school could see this."

"I'm not sure I'd call that flying," Scratchet chuckled. "But we didn't hit the ground, so it's something like it."

"I never dreamed in a million years this would ever happen to me," Maya huffed, still out of breath and shaking.

"Well, it's not over yet," I said in the calmest voice I could. I tried to sound as brave as possible, but secretly, I could very easily have cried at that moment. "Which way to the hop-spital, Maya?"

"Erm," our human friend thought for a second then pointed across the town square. "Over there; we need to go left around Bargain Land."

"Then what are we waiting for?" Scratchet cooed. She gave a tug on Blitzen's reins. "Head right, Blitzen! Don't go, girl!"

And just like that, we scudded off across the rooftops of Trudgeworth, dipping and weaving through the night air as we went, and trying very hard not to fall back out of it.

"That's it," Maya said after we'd nearly reached the outskirts of the sprawling town beneath us.

I looked to where our friend was pointing and saw a vast, modern building with brightly lit windows and a line of yellow-and-green vehicles that kept coming and going from the front of it.

"It's huge!" Scratchet gasped. "I thought it would be all piddly and small, like the elf-matron's hut back at the factory."

"There are lots of people who need help," Maya sighed.

"There must be thousands of people in there," Scratchet went on. "How can we bring Christmas to that many people all at once, Gris?"

I was glad that Scratchet and Maya were sitting in front of me in Blitzen's saddle. I hadn't actually thought that far ahead.

"We'll see what we can do," I muttered, trying to sound confident. "Where does your mum work, Maya?"

"She's on the children's ward, over there on the far corner," said Maya, gesturing to a wing that jutted out from the main building. "If we fly closer, I can show you."

With a lot of confusing commands and rein jerking, Scratchet managed to guide our wonk-witted reindeer towards a row of windows near the very top of the hop-spital. Hovering slowly towards them, until Blitzen hit the wall with soft thump.

"Another brilliant landing," my sister said sarcastically.

"Keep your noise down," I hissed as we found ourselves right in front of the glass. I couldn't help but feel nervous. "We mustn't be spotted."

"This is my mum's ward. It's been super busy lately," Maya said in a hushed voice.

"Whoa, it's nothing like the elf-matron's hut," whispered Scratchet, peering inside. "It's so … clean!"

We were looking at a large gloomy room filled with rows of beds, and in each one there slept a human child.

"What's wrong with them all?" Scratchet asked, counting the snoozing figures with a pointed finger.

"Lots of different things," Maya replied.

"And your mum takes care of all of them?" I said in amazement. "How incredibump!"

"No, not just my mum. She's part of a team, but there aren't enough of them. That's why they have to work at Christmas."

"It's not fair," said Scratchet. "And kidlies can't get better in such a miserable space. Your poor mumsy is fighting a losing battle."

"What do you mean?" I glanced at Scratchet and wondered what she was thinking. "Maybe you—"

Just then, a man and two women in blue uniforms walked into the room. The man had a mask over his nose and mouth, so it was difficult to tell much about him, but one of the ladies was tall and had lovely red curly hair, while the other was...

"That's your mum!" I cheered a little too loudly.

"Yep, there she is." Maya beamed. "I wish Mum could come on a reindeer ride with us."

We watched as the nurses rushed about. They were busier than lemmings tidying their burrows. They checked charts, tucked in blankets, fiddled with doohickeys, administered medicine, soothed a child who woke up from a bad dream, and darted back and forth until we were all dizzy. One thing was certain about all of them, including Maya's mummy ... they all seemed exhausterated.

"So, do you think you can do something to help?" asked Maya after a long silence, looking hopeful.

"I don't know ... umm ... Scratchet?" I mumbled. "Maybe ... err ... maybe..."

My sister looked at me blankly.

"Could you make the children all better, so Maya's mummy could come home for Christmas?" I went on. "With your magic, I mean?"

"Ugh!" Scratchet scowled at me, and for a second,

I thought she was going to push me straight off Blitzen's back. "You're just like Old Wimbles, d'you know that, Gris? Such a typical male elf!"

"What?" I exclaimed, trying to sound like I didn't know exactly what she was talking about.

"So, you announce the grand plan of coming here to spread some Christmas magic, but when we arrive, your idea is just to get me to do everything?"

"It's not my fault!" I tried to sound as innocent as possible. "You just ... well ... you're just so much better at it than anyone else."

Scratchet rolled her eyes at me, then turned back to Maya at the front of the saddle.

"Maya, I can't heal anyone. There's no elf-magic that can make those poorly children better. That's what your mumsy is for. Nurses are much more powerful than anything I can do."

"Oh..." Maya looked dejected. "That's OK."

"I'm sorry." Scratchet shot me a glance. It was angry at first, but then it softened and a smile crept in at the corner of her mouth. "But we can certainly remind them how magical they already are."

Maya glanced up into Scratchet's eyes.

"Huh?"

"It's Christmas," Scratchet chuckled. "Poorly children and tired nurses shouldn't be left in that grubberous grey room to feel miserable, should they?"

I watched as my little sister placed her fingertips on the window glass.

"Wait for it…" she said, examining the nurses hurrying about. "Wait for it…"

We stared in total silence, until … a phoney-talky-stick on the back wall of the room started to ring and Maya's mum went to pick it up. She talked to someone on the other end of the line for a moment, then called the two other colleagues over to ask them something.

"Now!" Scratchet grunted.

Just as all three nurses had their backs to the ward, me and Maya gawped, watching as strands of flickering sparks drifted from Scratchet's hand and danced across the unhappy room like the northern lights. In an instant, bolts of tinsel draped themselves in loops across the walls, each child's drab grey blanket turned into a fluffy red duvet, candles flickered into existence along the nearby shelves, stockings stuffed with fruits appeared at the foot of every bed, a Christmas tree sprouted in the centre of the room with little baubles amongst its branches, and three large envelopes swooped out of nowhere and hit each of the nurses gently on the back.

Tears welled up in my eyes as I watched Maya's mum turn around to see what had tapped her and...

The three grown-ups reeled backwards, yelping in shock and delight, causing the children to wake from their snizzling and sit up, mouths agog. Even outside in the wind, we could hear whoops of happiness and merriment.

"Haha!" Maya guffawed. "It's wonderful! It's WONDERFUL!"

"No problem, my friend," Scratchet said, taking her fingers away from the glass. "Hooo, I feel a bit woozy. That was a big one."

My sister looked at me as she wobbled slightly in Blitzen's saddle and gave me a wink.

"I was impressed when you turned a mince pie into a lump of coal," I laughed. "I didn't know you had that kind of trick up your sleeve!"

"Neither did I," she replied, blinking dizzily.

I looked back into the room and saw that some of the children were hopping about on their beds, and the male and female nurses were spinning about beneath a cloud that had drifted across the ceiling, dusting the Christmas tree with snow ... and right in the middle of all this was Maya's mum.

She'd picked up the envelope that had flown into her back, opened it and was reading the card inside with a tearful smile.

"What did you write in it?" I asked Scratchet.

"The usual slobberchopsy stuff," she said with a contented smile. "The world is better because you're in it..."

# Chapter 24

## Cancelled!

*I*t was extremely early and still dark outside when I heard the familiar *CLUNK! CLICK!* of keys in the front door the following morning.

When we'd dropped Maya off at her gran and grandad's last night, she told us she wouldn't be able to visit until after breakfast time, so ... so ... who was this coming in before daylight?

"Oh, blunkers!" Scratchet scrambled to her knees, alert and wide awake in a flash. She looked at me across the sleeping bodies of our parents and grandparents and mouthed the words *"Mrs Pinkerton"* at me.

A shape ran down the darkened hallway, and I flinched, ready to dive under my blanket and play dead. But, just as I was thinking we'd been rumpled, Maya sprinted into the room looking panicked and out of breath.

"HUMBUGS!" she yelled, waking everybody in one go. I could tell something was terribly wrong. She was wearing her coat over her pyjamas and her shoes were both untied.

"Maya, what's happening?" Scratchet yelped, jumping to her feet. "What's going on?"

"It's everywhere!" Maya panted with wide eyes and messy hair. "I ran here as fast as I could. Grandad woke me up. The telly! It's all over the telly!"

"Wha's all this?" Old Wimbles croaked, flailing his arms and legs in the air like an upturned tortoise.

"It's that girl," Nana Pilchard grumbled as she hauled herself on to her elbows. "She's gone all fustery in the bonce-bits."

"Maya, we don't understand," I said as she stared

at us in alarm. "Tell us everything." I guided her into one of the chairs round the table, while Mum fetched some water from the runny-drippy-pipe.

"Here you are, my dunkling," Mum said softly, handing Maya a glass. She put a hand on the girl's forehead and waited. "Hmmm … you don't have a fever, but you do seem to have had a nasty shock. Did something bad happen to you?"

"Not me!" Maya cried; she looked like she might faint and fall off her seat. "It's you, Humbugs! You're all over the telly. It's on every channel around the world!"

"Wha-what!?" Dad blurted. "You mean the picture-thingy on the wall?"

"YES!"

"What are we waiting for?" Nana hobbled to her clankerous feet and thudded through the door between the food room and the not-a-real-tree room. "Where's the bonker?" she yelled, looking about frantically.

"The what?" Dad asked as he ran into the room behind her.

"The buzzer! The clicker-thinger!" Nana started miming using the remote to turn on the telly screen. "Where's the button-poker?"

"This?" Scratchet grabbed the gadget from the arm of the comfy-squishy-chair and pointed it at the black rectangle on the wall. Immediately the picture flickered to life and we saw ... we saw...

"SANTA!" everyone blurted in unison.

"What's that gribbly old lump doin' on the telly-box?" Nana bawled.

We all fell silent and watched the breaking news as it unfolded in front of us and a reporter appeared on the screen. She was dressed in a neat blue suit and her hair was all billowy like well-combed candy-floss.

"Hello, ladies and gentlemen," she announced to the camera with an extremely grave expression. "My name is Valerie Bunston and we have shocking news for you on this Christmas Eve morning. We're now going live to the North Pole, via satellite link, to speak to Santa Claus himself at the Christmas Factory."

A square appeared over Valerie Bunston's shoulder

and we could clearly see Santa Claus peering into the news camera lens.

"Now, Santa," Valerie went on, "there have been some concerning reports coming from the North Pole about problems in the toy workshops – what can you tell us about this?"

Santa looked into the camera and twiddled nervously with the end of his beard.

I have to admit that I wasn't fond of this current Santa. His name was Percy Claus, sixteenth great-grandson of Nikolaus, and he was far more lazy than some who had gone before him. Nana was convinced he was a snively drip-lip, and I couldn't disagree with her.

"Erm ... hello ... hello, Valerie," Santa stammered. He looked more uncomfortable than a polar bear in the Bahamas. "Yes, I'm afraid it's true."

"There are problems in your Christmas Factory?" Valerie questioned.

"Worse than problems, I'm sorry to say," Santa said with a trembling jaw. "There's pandemonium here. It's all ground to a halt. EVERYTHING!"

"So, what are you telling us exactly?" Valerie leaned in close to the camera. "What is it you've come on the morning news to explain?"

"It is with sadness and a heavy heart that I have to tell the world ... well ... erm..."

"Go on, Mr Claus," Valerie pushed him. "Please continue."

"I have to tell the world..." Santa was getting pinker and pinker by the second. A large bead of sweat dripped off the end of his nose. "... CHRISTMAS IS CANCELLED THIS YEAR!"

"What the blunkin' boogles!?" Nana Pilchard gasped. "Have my ears gone make-believy?"

"It can't be true," Mum sobbed. "What on earth has happened, do you think?"

"Maybe there's a bug going around the workshop?" Dad thought out loud. "Or ... umm ... could the workshop machinery have broken?"

We all turned back to the telly-box.

"This is SCANDALOUS news, Mr Claus!" Valerie Bunston exclaimed.

"It's not my fault," Santa whined.

"Well, perhaps you'd like to let the people of the world know exactly what's happening up at the North Pole?"

"Erm … I'd rather not … if it's all the same to—"

Suddenly, Mrs Claus appeared in the background and prodded her husband in the shoulder.

"You tell them right now, or I'll put YOU on your own naughty list," she snapped.

"Yes, dear," Santa whimpered. "Sorry." He turned back towards the camera, took a deep breath and… "It started a few days ago when my head foreman, Bungustus McMerrypie, may have fired a family of workers and banished them out into the frozen white waste of the Arctic tundra…"

"THEY'RE TALKING ABOUT US!" Scratchet screamed. She grabbed the button-gadget and turned the volume on the telly-box up even louder.

"We're going to be stars and all famousy, I bet," Nana rasped a laugh.

"Listen," pleaded Dad. "They're saying more!"

"Go on, Santa," Valerie said, glaring dramatically into the camera.

"And ... well ... that family worked in the R.P.D. department."

"Which is?" Valerie raised an eyebrow sternly.

"It's a bit rude," Santa mumbled, blushing even pinker. "It means ... umm..."

"OH, JUST GET OUT THE WAY!" Mrs Claus shoved her husband aside and positioned herself in full view of the news camera instead of him. "MEN!" she grunted, and rolled her eyes.

Valerie sat up, looking a little alarmed by the change of interviewee.

"Mrs Claus, perhaps you can shed a little more light on the subject."

"Call me Mavis," Mrs Claus said, smiling. "No one around here will ever use my first name and I'm sick of being Mrs Claus all the time. Mrs Claus this... Mrs Claus that... It's like I'm just attached to him. A spare part, if you will."

"Mavis," Valerie corrected herself. "Tell us everything."

"Truth is, Valerie, those workshop elves have been spoiled for years. Right snobbly little blighters, some of 'em. Always going after the glory and never the actual joy of making a little kiddy-winkle's Christmas extra magical. So ... they look down their noses at any other elf who works around here, and the other little duckies get fired and sent off for the simplest of things! Long story short, this R.P.D. family – R.P.D. stands for Reindeer Poo Disposal, by the way – this family has been sent off and everything's stopped without 'em!"

"What are you saying, Mavis?" Valerie quizzed. "Are you saying the factory has been inundated with ... erm ... reindeer poo?"

"No! Nothing like that, although if you give those mangy beasts half a chance they would. They're poo-machines, honestly! Anyway, the great furnaces that power the factory are fuelled by the reindeer poo around here, and with no one to rake and shovel it, the fires have gone out."

"And what does this mean for the rest of the factory?"

"Well, Valerie" – Mrs Claus was really ramping herself up for her grand finale – "without the furnaces, the sleighworks and bake house have no power. That means no repairs in the garage, and no mince pies from the ovens. Without any mince pies, the workshop snobblers can't cope because they're all so spoiled and scoffley, and there's no hot water for Santa's bubble baths, and he's a right whinge-bucket without those. It's chaos! No one's working and we can't find the Humbugs anywhere…"

Scratchet turned the telly-box off and we all froze in silence for what seemed like an eternity. No one spoke … no one breathed … no one until…

"HAHA! That's the best news I've ever heard!" Nana Pilchard clapped her stumpy hands and rocked back and forth on the arm of the comfy-squishy-chair.

"We have to go back!" I blurted.

"Not on your nelly," Nana Pilchard yelled back at me. "I'm not going back to that muck-dump. They deserve everything they get, the weasly whelpers!"

"But…"

"No buts, young Gristle," Old Wimbles shut me up. "We're not going back to that worky, no-thanksy life, no sirree!"

"But Christmas is depending on us!" I yelled. "If we don't return, no child around the world will get their presents from Santa. In some places it's the only present they'll get at all."

"You heard your friend here," Nana pointed at Maya. "Kids don't care about presents any more. They've got everything they want already."

"You're missing the point!" Arguing with Nana and Old Wimbles was SO frustrating, but I had to make them listen. A fire exploded in my belly and I scrunched my toes, clenched my bumly-bits and hoped for the best. "For centuries, I thought the only things that mattered in the Christmas Factory were the toys. Toys for everyone! I longed to be a toymaker and live at the workshops, but you're right, Nana, the toys themselves don't matter. It's the fact that someone made an effort. That's what really means something. When each child gets a gift, they know that Santa and his elves did that just for them, regardless of what the gift is. It's the same with everything we've seen in Trudgeworth. It doesn't matter if the carollers are singing flat notes, or people get stressed doing the shopping, or the Christmas tree isn't real, or the dinner is burnt, or your parents have to work late, because everyone has made an effort. It's an act of love, and that's why we have to go back! Just like Maya's mum, we work hard, and we get tired, and we don't get appreciated or paid enough, and we complain sometimes, but we do it because we're helping people and … and … we're Humbugs … and…" Tears were streaming down my face. I looked up and saw that everyone in my family was blubbing too. "And that's the real heart of Christmas."

What can I say, my human reader? I'm an emotional elf at times.

It didn't take long for us to gather our belongings and lead Blitzen down to the dark carp ark. Maya came with us, and I couldn't shake the guilty feeling that we'd ruined her Christmas after all.

"I didn't expect all this," I muttered, while we waited for Dad to harness the reindeer into place at the front of our trusty dumpster. "I wanted to make this your best Christmas ever."

"Don't worry, Gristle," said Maya. "You've already done that, and now Mum won't forget it EVER! You have to save Christmas for everyone ... that's plenty for one elf to deal with."

"We'll come back," I said. "One day."

"Really?" Maya asked.

"I promise. If we hadn't found your letter, and spoiled your Christmas, and come to visit, I never would have realized that ... that..."

"That you were worth a lot more than toys and tidy jerkins," Scratchet said from behind me. "I always knew it, brother."

I turned to my sister and she gave me a sad smile.

"It's time to go," she said.

Over Scratchet's shoulder, I could see my family were all waiting patiently in the dumpster with Blitzen snuffling about in front.

"Come on then," I said. "Goodbye, Maya Pinkerton."

"Bye, Gristle," Maya said quietly. "Bye, Scrachet."

"Oh, hang on!" Scratchet huffed. "There's one last thing..."

We all watched as she walked up to the nearest wall of Greymarsh Tower and placed her hand upon it, just like she'd done to the hop-spital window.

"I'm not sure I can do this properly, but I've got a bit of elf-magic that's tingled in my fingertips ever since last night." Scratchet said. "Give me space, this is a lot bigger than one room."

She scrunched up her eyes, gave a little growl of concentration, and...

"What's happening?" Maya gasped as vines seemed to suddenly start sprouting out of Scratchet's hand, spreading quickly all over the surface of the building.

"Just you watch." Scratchet giggled. "I can't believe it's actually working."

Squiggly stems rapidly surrounded each window, crept up the walls in zigzag lines, and formed spiral shapes around the entrance. They were growing faster and faster until they reached all the way up to the roof, high above us.

"Are they plants?" asked Maya when the spindly lines finally stopped wriggling and Scratchet removed her hand from the wall.

"Not quite," Scratchet replied. She gave one last flick of her wrist and a million colourful lights twinkled across Greymarsh Tower, making it look like a mirage.

"Fairy lights!" Maya whooped. "Thank you, it looks wonderful!"

"Fairy lights?" Scratchet baulked at the words in mock disgust. "I think you'll find they're elf lights, Maya, and you're very welcome indeed…"

# Chapter 25

## The Elf Who Saved Christmas

Snow and wind whipped our faces as Blitzen dragged our dumpster through the Arctic sky.

"We've got to go quicker," Mum worried and fussed. "It's Christmas Eve. There's no time!"

"Don't get your baubles bunched, Flotsima," Nana yelled over the gale that was blowing straight against us. "Blister's doing the best she can."

Ahead, I could see the green smudge of the Northern Lights, and ... I couldn't tell if my eyes were playing tricks on me, but there seemed to be a warm glow coming into view amongst the craggy ice and snow below us.

"Look!" I shouted, pointing over Nana's shoulder. As it came into clearer focus, I could make out the unmistakeable shape of the Big House, the looming mass of the sleighworks and the steeply pointed roofs of the Great Letter Hall.

"I never thought I'd see the place again," Old Wimbles wheezed in the icy air. "Time flies, as they say ... feels like only days have passed."

"Pops, it has only been days," Scratchet corrected him.

"But a lot can change in a little while," Nana said. Her face looked set and resolute. "I think it's time we paid Santa Claus a visit."

She gave Blitzen's reins an almighty yank, hollering *"UP!"* at the frantically flying beast, and Blitzen dramatically nosedived towards the factory.

We swooped over the smokeless bake house chimneys and rounded the bandstand in the plaza as elves dashed outside from all over, pointing and cheering. I wanted to feel angry or upset about returning. I wanted not to care about the upturned faces gawping at us after we were thrown out and Bungustus McMerrypie and his cronies were so rude, but the truth is, I was giddy with gladness to see it all again.

"There they are," Dad bellowed. He gestured to the loading veranda in front of the Big House and sure enough, there, next to the toy-laden sleigh was Santa, surrounded by a gaggle of workshop elves.

"DON'T LAND HERE, BLISTER!" Nana squawked, and Blitzen brought the dumpster down with violent bump right next to where the sour-faced elves were all gathered. Several of them screamed and dived out of the way as we plummeted into view and Santa sprawled against the side of his sleigh like his bones had turned to jelly.

"We're under attack!" Scurrily Pudgenut screeched as she cowered behind Santa's leg.

"Is it outsiders, come to steal from us?" Primpy Patonk sobbed.

"Monsters?" Ariazmus Bunt wailed, hiding his face with one of his books.

Nana raised her stolen flying goggles on to her forehead, wedged her fists against her hips and scowled.

"It's worse than that, you bunch of scruzzlies." She clambered out of the dumpster with about as much balance as a drunken elephant, straightened herself up, and strutted towards the juddered little crowd, trying to look as intimidating as possible ... which wasn't difficult for someone like Nana Pilchard.

"What's all this I've been hearing about the factory cancelling Christmas this year?" she snapped.

"Mrs Humbug, is that you?" Bungustus McMerrypie gasped. "But ... we thought you were out there, lost to the frozen white waste. We thought you might have popped your clonkers."

"It'll take much more than a bit of snow and ice to defeat me and my family," Nana roared. It was very impressive, even if I say so myself. "What have you got to say for yourself, Santa?"

"Me?" Santa snivelled. "I didn't do anything. It was Bungustus who sent you away!"

"No … you didn't do anything. You didn't bother to come out and see my little Gristle and Scratchet when they found some missing mail and saved the day either! And now it looks like you're not doing anything to save Christmas!"

"You can't speak to me like that," Santa blurted. He looked utterly stunned that any elf would dare to stand their ground in front of him.

"Oh, can't I, you lilly-lumping useless bogbag?" Nana stamped her foot and Scurrily Pudgenut fainted.

"It's not my fault!" Santa was hopping up and down with panic. "There was simply nothing to be done."

"He's right," Crotchety Humpkins said in a sickly whisper, fanning herself with the back of her hands. "It was chaos; there were elves screaming and running all over the place. The furnaces went out, the ovens stopped, the sleighworks went dark! Our mince pies stopped arriving at the workshop and we … we … we PRACTICALLY STARVED!"

"You've got plenty of other food," Nana scoffed at the melodramatic moaner.

"I know," Crotchety said. Her voice was barely a croak. "We already ate it."

"And there's an endless supply of pine needles around for boiling," Dad called. "That would have kept you going."

"Eurgh, we're not eating muck!" Jinkly Rolly-Poll whinged from her gaggle of elves.

"Why didn't you ask the Gardyloos or the LaTrines to fuel the furnaces? They're still around, aren't they? You didn't banish them too?" Mum asked as she climbed down from the dumpster, followed by me and Scratchet.

"We did ... they're very unmotivated," Santa mumbled. "They told us to ... bog off."

"HAHA!!" Nana Pilchard slapped her knee and guffawed merrily. "WHAT DID I TELL YOU, FLOTSIMA? I'm always right. That Gazunder Gardyloo is a right napster. The Humbugs win again!"

"Fine," Mum shrugged, ignoring Nana. "But, why couldn't any of you workshoppers just carry some reindeer poo to the furnace yourself? You're all perfectly capable."

"Carry poo?" Jinkly Rolly-Poll spat the words at Mum like darts. "That kind of work is for…" She thought for a moment and her mouth puckered into a vinegary smile. "That work is for *different* elves. We're not different, so we shouldn't have to do it."

"I agree," Crotchety Humpkins piped-up, suddenly not so weak and frail.

"Me too!" Primpy Patonk stuck her tongue out at Nana and I felt my whole family freeze with anticipation. Only the most foolish of fools would dare to do something so … erm … FOOLISH in front of Pilchard P. Humbug.

"RIGHT!" Nana looked like she was about to go berserk. I may be remembering this wrongly, but I could swear there were flames coming out of her nostrils, my reader friend … maybe not … but she balled her hands into fists, spread her feet wide and thundered, "You'd better shut your goblets, and shut 'em good! I'll have you know that while we've been away, my lovelish family of *different* elves visited the human world."

"Lies!" Crotchety Humpkins laughed.

"TRUTH!" Nana roared back, making Miss Humpkins recoil like she'd just touched her snooty nose to something hot. "My Gristle took us all on a very squibbly holly-day. We've seen all sorts of humans and places and Taj Mahals. Loads of 'em! We chatted with nurses, and ate breakfast with kiddlies, saw a man selling hot and sizzly dogs, and we frightened someone named Greg Bottley! How about that!?"

Santa and his cronies stared blankly, looking extremely confused.

"Nana." I stepped nearer, feeling a little nervous to be this close to the tiny tornado. "I think you might be wandering away from the subject."

"I'm doing no such thing!" Nana grunted and rolled up her cardigan sleeves. "I'm being very clear."

"So, what's your point, outsider?" Jinkly Rolly-Poll jeered.

"My point," Nana Pilchard barked. "Is we're all blunkin' different, you brain-scrumbled nitwonk! I've been alive for more years than you've scuffled down mince pies, and all I ever see is you workshoppers whiffly-waffling over the rest of us. You could have carried some reindeer poo to the furnaces, but you just didn't want to. You didn't want to make the effort … and effort is … well … erm … Christmas and effort are … erm…"

Nana turned to me and pulled me forward before the affronted elves.

"You're better at wordsy stuff than me, Gristle," she said. "I get all tongue-twizzled. Tell 'em what you told us."

I looked at each of the workshoppers in turn and tried to steady my nerves. Only a few days ago these people had been my heroes. Now they seemed like wretched bullies.

"My nana is right," I said as my stomach did a cartwheel. I tried to remember what I'd said earlier at Greymarsh Tower. *Courage, Gristle, courage.* "Christmas spirit is only real when someone tries hard. Even a tiny, wonky, blustery or clumsy effort is a wonderfus thing. It's how we show love. Before we left the factory, I thought the only thing that mattered were toys. But it's not true. A hug is worth a thousand toys. Trains and dolls and building blocks are great, they make children happy, but they have nothing to do with the real meaning of Christmas. No one should be thought of as more important around here because they live and work in the Big House. You, Crotchety Humpkins, and Bungustus McMerrypie, and even you, Santa ... any one of you could have kept the furnaces going, but you didn't want to get your hands dirty. None of you have any Christmas spirit..." I couldn't believe these words were coming out of the jabbering hole in my head. "You're all ... you're all ... CRUSTY LUMPS OF COAL!"

There was an intense moment of angry silence. I suddenly worried that I may have gone too far, until...

"*YEEEEEEAAAAAAHHHHHH!*"

I spun around and nearly fell over with surprise. While I'd been so intently focused on Santa and his mean elves, the plaza had slowly filled to bursting point. There were throngs of elves! More even than the day me and Scratchet found Maya Pinkerton's letter, and they were all cheering for ... for us!

I looked out over the factory compound and felt a little something shift in the air … in me, maybe? I can't put my finger on quite what it was, but I knew things would never go back to the way they were before.

As I watched the factory elves whooping and cheering, I noticed there was one voice that was louder than all the rest.

Turning back around to the Big House, I looked up and saw Mrs Claus hurrying down the spiral staircase from the private apartments above the workshop.

"Bravo, kiddo!" she cried, and an audible wave of chatter went out across the factory.

"Bless my bunions!" huffed Nana Pilchard. "Mrs Claus, it's a whoppsy honour, it is."

Mum and Dad were next to me in a flash.

"Oh, you Humbugs are a breath of fresh and frosty air." Mrs Claus laughed as she reached the veranda and greeted us. "I heard every word of what you said, young … Gristle, was it?"

"Yes," I mumbled. Mrs Claus was actually speaking to me!

"Well, I think you're absolutely right, Gristle. I couldn't agree more."

Santa sidled up next to his wife, looking somewhere between peeing his fluffy red trousers and crying.

"Erm … darling … I don't think you should say such things in front of…"

"In front of your little gaggle of gossips?" Mrs Claus interrupted. She turned back to me. "Between you and me, Gristle, and everybody else here, Bungustus McMerrypie is a blustering windbag and those three" – she pointed to Crotchety Humpkins, Jinkly Rolly-Poll and Primpy Patonk – "are meaner than rattlesnakes."

"But I can't be mean! Or wrong!" Jinkly Rolly-Poll wailed. "I'm famous!"

"Oh, zip it!" Mrs Claus shot back at her.

"Erm … darling…" Santa said, looking more and more panic-stricken.

"You can zip it as well," Mrs Claus said to her husband. "Now I want you to face your elves. All of them … and tell them exactly how you're going to fix this mess."

Santa didn't do anything.

"Go on!" Mrs Claus gave him a gentle nudge with her elbow.

"Erm..." Santa slowly turned to face me with eyes full of bewilderment. I wasn't sure what he was going to say, but his hand started reaching up for the red hat with white trim that perched on his head, and ... "You take it," he said.

"What!?" I felt like someone had just biffed me in the stomach.

"I don't want to do it any more," Santa snivelled. "I don't like snow, and I don't like toys, and I don't even like mince pies! I ... I ... I WANT A HOLIDAY!"

Everyone was utterly flabbergusted. Even Mrs Claus looked surprised.

"Take it, boy," Santa said, and held the hat towards me. "You'll be the boss of the whole factory. You can eat pastries and order everyone around."

"That's not what I meant," I said, trying to stop my knees from shaking. "No, Santa ... I don't want it."

"But..." Santa looked at me like I was the

stupidest thing in the universe. "You can be in charge of everything!"

"GIVE IT 'ERE!"

We all watched as Nana Pilchard shuffled over and took the famous red hat from Santa. She looked at it for a second, cooed to herself and plopped it on to her scraggly head.

"Righty-ho." She rubbed the palms of her calloused hands together and grinned mischievously. "Let's be 'avin yer."

# Secret Chapter 26

## One Year Later...

So ... there you have it, my human reader. That's the story of how Nana Pilchard saved Christmas.

What?!? You didn't think the title of this book was about me, did you? Nana was practically born for the job of a Santa. She had the factory back up and running in a jiffy, although she made a few small changes.

From that moment onwards, nobody belonged to any single department. Everyone had the chance to try the jobs they wanted – and the jobs they didn't want so much as well. There wasn't a single elf who couldn't enjoy the fun of making toys and feel the drudge of shovelling reindeer poo too. Even Bungustus, and Crotchety, and all her mean pals had to pull their weight around the stables!

Nana's first order was for the bake house to make thousands more mince pies than they'd ever baked before and everyone was very excited, certain they'd be getting a chance to feast this year.

Before we knew it, everything was quickly back on track and ready for that evening's Great Delivery Run. The giant Christmas sleigh was readied with a team of elite reindeer, led by – you guessed it – Blister! Nana insisted we all call her by her official name from now on.

Throngs of elves gathered along the airstrip that evening to see the first ever female Santa Claus get ready for take-off, and it was just as she clambered into the driver's seat, right before she soared into the great beyond that Nana made her big speech.

"I'M KNACKERED!"

Yep! Nana Pilchard will for ever go down in history as not only the first female Santa, but also the shortest serving Santa as well.

The entire factory watched in total bafflement as Nana yanked off the famous red hat, and turned to me.

"Santa should be someone youngly and ready for the adventure, Gristle, my dunkling. Do it for Nana? My feet feel like blockbunkles."

I swear I'd never felt so swirly and confuserated in my whole life, my human reader. I'd already turned the job down once, but I will admit there was a tingle of exhilaration at being given a second try. With a thousand thoughts racing through me, I reached up, took the hat, and...

"Good on you, Gristle! I'm proud of you!"

It was my little sister. Brilliant, astonishing, wildly courageous Scratchet.

Everything became clear all at once.

"I'm not the one to lead the Great Delivery Run," I announced to the anticipating crowds. "It's not me you need." Then I turned to Scratchet and placed the hat on her head.

"Good on *YOU*, Scratchet." I beamed, with tears in my eyes. "I'm proud of *you*."

And that, my human reader, is the story of how Scratchet saved Christmas. Haha! You couldn't have believed that Nana Pilchard would have the energy to fly around the world in one night, could you? If she'd gone out on the Great Delivery Run, Nana would have dumped all the toys in the ocean and been back in five minutes ready for her nap!

Scratchet P. Humbug, the youngest Santa ever to take on the job, leapt into action. She already knew Nana Pilchard's plans for tonight's operation, and before you could blink, she was clambering into the sleigh ready to make her first factory-wide speech. I prayed it would be longer than Nana's...

Thankfully it was...

"My elvish friends," she called over the thousands of assembled elves. "This year we're doing things a smidge different. We all got grumpsy and lazy around here, so we've got an idea to make up for it. This year, instead of presents, we're giving each and every human, adults included, one of our North Pole mince pies. Proper bake house ones, not the rubbish things they have in shops. Our pies are made with love and we'll pass it on to the humans. We'll go without our pastries to show that we care, and to remind the world that toys are not the meaning of Christmas."

Scratchet turned around and flung open the enormous sack in the back of the sleigh, revealing it was filled with squillions of crumbly and delicious pies.

"But what about all the toys?" an elf from the ribbon dispensary cried out.

"I've already thought of that," Scratchet declared. She waved a signal and Swilsy Plumpaunch rattled out on to the airstrip in his postal cart filled with teddy bears, dolls, books, puzzles, games and building blocks.

"The pie-piggling workshoppers didn't make enough toys for the whole world this year, but we'll put the ones we've got to good use." Scratchet went on. "These are all going to Trudgeworth Hop-spital, and all the other hop-spitals around the planet. Those little poorly pluglets deserve 'em most."

Watching from a little way off, I didn't know it was possible to feel so honoured to be related to somebody.

"We'll fix Christmas and remind the workers of the world that we see them!"

With that, Scratchet sat down in the great big front seat, lowered the stolen goggles that she'd retrieved from Nana, and yelled, "DON'T DASH, BLISTER!" and away they went.

Since then, Scratchet has revolutionized the Christmas Factory. It's true!

After learning about all the telly-boxes and talky-phone-sticks in the human world, she dismantled all the big smoky furnaces in the bake house and replaced them with fancy ovens instead, powered by beautiful windmills on all the roofs.

But that left us with a problem, my human reader. If we weren't burning reindeer poo any more, the factory needed to come up with an ingenious way of using it – and indeed we did.

Scratchet got rid of all the coal. "*Nasty, dirty bits of blot-dots,*" she called it, and she found a clever replacement.

So, even though the toy workshops are back up and running smoothly this year … ahem … if you were naughty over the last twelve months and ended up on THE LIST, you can expect a box containing a certain stinky little nugget as a gift on Christmas morning. With love from the R.P.D. Department. Haha! Don't blame me ... it's got to go somewhere...

Things really are humdifferous around here these days. Mum and Dad still work in the stables, but they now train up new teams of poo shovellers and have their very own little cottage in the yard with a bath and comfy bed. Nana Pilchard mostly dodders about in the bake house kitchens, Old Wimbles spends most of his time in the private apartments at the Big House watching his very own telly-box, and Scratchet? Well ... she changed history.

Anyway, I'm nattering on when I've got run!

Maya and her mum are coming on holly-day to the factory this year and we promised we'd show them around the place.

But, before I go, let me remind you... If this strange little story had a message, it would be to hug your friends and family when you can, be mischievous, dare to dream great big bungly dreams, remember that giving expensive things is not the same as caring, know that unkindness will always result in you receiving poo, and always try to show love for those who work hard behind the scenes just to make our lives a little bit nicer. The world is better because you're in it!

# MERRY CHRISTMAS!!

# My Christmas List

# Nice Things I've Done
# This Year

_____

_____

_____

_____

_____

_____

_____

_____

_____

_____

_____

_____

# Christmas Gift Ideas For The Heroes In My Life

_____

_____

_____

_____

_____

_____

_____

_____

_____

_____

_____

_____

# Acknowledgements

A huge thank you to my FABULOUS team at Scholastic. Kenneth Anderson, your artwork made this book look SO beautiful! I am incredibly grateful. Ruth Bennett, it was so lovely to work with you, plotting-out Gristle's adventure right from the beginning. Lauren Fortune and Yasmin Morrissey, you guys are the dream team! I've never laughed and cried in such equal measure while editing a book. Hannah Love, you're definitely not getting reindeer poo for Christmas. Thank you for publicising Humbug so brilliantly. Thank you, thank you, thank you!

Armfuls of gratitude to my nearest and dearest. Jenny Gyertson, Steven Lenton, Francesca Simon, Filip Krenus, Kirsten Grant! You've all kept me sane and feeling very loved while I stressed and bungled my way through Humbug (sometimes muttering some not very festive things about Christmas under my breath).

And finally, to every key-worker out there ... the valiant NHS staff, the drivers, the cleaners, the carers, the cooks, the teachers, the booksellers, the deliverers and everyone who kept us ticking along, safe and hopeful, through the past few years. You all deserve A LOT of mince pies.

*Steven Butler* is an award-winning and NY Times bestselling author, performer and voice artist. His books have won the coveted *Sainsbury's Children's Book Award*, and been shortlisted for the *Roald Dahl Funny Prize*, *Alligator's Mouth Award* and the *Lollies*. When he isn't writing **really funny** books, Steven splits his time between obsessing about spices and cooking in his tiny London kitchen, and spending time in Brighton with his pet dog, Big-Eared Bob (which is his full name).

Steven is a dedicated fan of all things Christmas, and a firm believer in the joyful power of mince pies. ***Humbug: The Elf Who Saved Christmas*** is his first Christmas novel – and his **FUNNIEST** Christmas novel!